SCOTTISH GHOSTS

LILY SEAFIELD

WAVERLEY BOOKS

Published 2009 by Waverley Books,
David Dale House, New Lanark, ML11 9DJ, Scotland

© 2009 Waverley Books

ISBN 978 1902407 86 9

Printed and bound in the UK

CONTENTS

INTRODUCTION

Scotland is a country with a rich and varied history, a land of strikingly beautiful scenery with a people proud of its traditions and heritage. The years that have passed since the beginnings of its history have seen much conflict and upheaval and many triumphs and tragedies that absorb historians and capture the imaginations of storytellers and their audiences. Scottish folk legends tell of fairies, giants and monsters that have lived (or still do live) cheek by jowl with the mere mortals who inhabit this small country. Where or why these stories began no one can be certain, but they have entertained audience and teller alike for many long years and continue to do so. Whether such stories have any base in fact is a matter for debate, but there will always be those who believe that they have some truth attached to them. The search for the Loch Ness Monster goes on, for example, and probably will for all time.

It is the same with the many hundreds of ghosts that are said to populate Scotland. It seems that wherever you go, whatever stories you hear about a place and its past, there is likely to be a ghost story lurking in the background, ready for anyone who will listen. The spectres of sinners condemned to a life in eternal limbo, the tortured souls of those who have been shamefully wronged, victims of cruel and terrible crimes, mysterious 'green ladies', 'white ladies' and phantoms determined to leave their mark on the living, soldiers, animals and ghastly deformed creatures, all have their place in Scottish ghost stories. Old ghosts, new ghosts, Scotland has them all, ready for those who are willing to hear them, see them or sense their presence. Some ghosts have the ability, it would appear, not only to delight the committed ghost-hunter but also to convince the most sceptical of unbelievers. There are plenty of accounts of people who have been shocked into believing in the existence of ghosts by the appearance of just such a thing, making their hair stand on end and sending them screaming, white-faced, from their beds.

To those who remain dubious, it is clear why some ghost stories have been told. Perhaps a place has a great history of colourful characters who performed gory deeds. The history makes good telling, but people want to hear more. These colourful characters are dead, so what more can be said? The thing to do is to keep them going in ghostly form: a creak in the night, the howl of the wind, a falling leaf brushing past a face – these things can all take on sinister form and be attributed to the mischief of those who have gone before. History comes alive again and is so much more exciting; people will flock to hear the stories and share in the experience.

Other ghost stories, the unbelievers will tell you, are merely the product of over-fertile imaginations. Someone was wakened in the night? It was no more than a bad dream. A shiver down the spine? There must be some normal physiological explanation. And so it goes on. But the tales of supernatural occurrences multiply. Sometimes a rational explanation simply cannot be found. Evidence has been collected of people's experiences and stories have been compared. Books have been written. Television documentaries have been made. Ghosts have really made the big time – and Scotland is full of them.

This book contains details of many of the most famous of Scottish ghosts, some of which are hundreds of years old. It also tells of some that are not so well known and some that are not so old.

Some ghost stories are strikingly similar – older tales of ghosts and the supernatural that have become very much like the modern 'urban myth', perhaps because they have been passed from person to person so many times over many years. When an urban myth is told, it is almost always told as something that happened to a friend of a friend, or a relative of a friend. The events in the story are generally said to have taken place in the town or city in which the story is being told. The same story will undoubtedly have been told in several other places nationwide; each time it will be told as something that happened to somebody connected to the storyteller, in the town in which the story is being told. Thus the same story (details may vary but the content will be much the same) finds itself associated with several different locations and groups of people. Some ghost stories are like this – the same basic elements are there but the places and the people involved are different. It must be the case, therefore, that some of the stories will, quite simply, be untrue.

Some of the stories in this book are myths that have their roots in the nature and activities of the personality involved. The stories that were circulated about Bonnie Dundee are a prime example of this, as are the legends that surround Michael Scott of Balwearie. Bonnie Dundee was a figure who was both feared and hated by many people so it is perhaps not surprising that rumours about his supposed devilish associations and supernatural powers were circulated by his enemies. Michael Scott was by all accounts very clever and learned, and great learning can inspire fear and suspicion.

Some ghost stories, inevitably, have their origins in long, dark nights by the fire, when a gifted storyteller with a fertile imagination could easily send a chill down the spines of a willing audience.

In a country in which beliefs in many things supernatural have been widespread for so many years, it is inevitable that there will be many more stories than real supernatural occurrences. This book makes no attempt to separate fact from fancy. Those readers who wish to pursue their interest in the ghosts and supernatural beings of Scotland can follow their own trail. This book can act as a starting point, but each ghost-hunter will find him or herself following a different path. There are so many ghosts and so many stories to chase.

In addition to the stories of particular ghosts and eerie happenings, mention is made of some of the beliefs that people in Scotland held, and sometimes still hold, about supernatural phenomena of various kinds – the nameless supernatural 'types' that were thought to visit the world of mere mortals, influencing them and sometimes playing havoc with their lives. The devil has also earned his place in this book, for he has been associated with many of the ghostly tales of evil deeds and strange occurrences after death that were told all over Scotland over the years.

FAIRIES, GREEN LADIES AND DEVILISH STRUGGLES

Fairies

Scottish folklore is populated with a whole host of fairies, demons, ghosts, green ladies and other manifestations. It is hard, perhaps impossible, to separate these into distinct entities, for the stories and beliefs that relate to them are closely intertwined. For example, the fairy and the ghost were much the same according to certain traditions. Some fairies were not so much perceived as 'little people' but rather as spirits of people long dead, either imprisoned on earth or left on earth after having been denied entrance to either heaven or hell. Some fairies were believed to be evildoers and mischief-makers, abducting women and children; others were less malevolent, granting wishes and effecting changes for the better in the lives of the mortals who crossed their paths.

Human interaction with the fairy world was fraught with problems. There was always the danger that if you crossed a fairy the consequences could be unpleasant in the extreme. Thus, there are stories of people who have discovered a magic salve that, if rubbed on their eyes, helps them to see fairies. When this facility is discovered by someone in the fairy kingdom, the mortal concerned at the very least has the facility taken away, but more often will have the offending eye or eyes put out.

There are countless tales of people who have seen into the world, or kingdom, of the fairies, whether through gift, by chance, through the use of a magic salve or in a dream. Stories of people who have had such access to, or sight of, the world of the fairies often tell how a living person has looked into the fairy world and recognised relatives, friends or acquaintances who have died and are now living in the fairy realm. Tales such as these reinforce the idea of a link between the ghost or spirit of the dead and the fairy.

The fairy world, much like the world of the spirits, has its own time, which bears no relation to real time. This uniqueness of time, or perhaps timelessness, which is associated with fairyland, is illustrated by one particular story that comes from Inverness.

The story tells how two fiddlers were visiting Inverness, looking for places to perform, when they met an old man who asked them if they would play at a dance for him. This they agreed to, and they followed the old man to a place called Tomnahurich. They reached Tomnahurich, a small hill outside Inverness, towards nightfall. They entered a opening in the side of the hill and found themselves in a richly decorated hall where scenes of great merriment were taking place. A party was well under way, with food and wine laid on in astonishing quality and abundance. The fiddlers found themselves in the company of many beautiful, but very small and fine-boned, women. The men were allowed to eat and drink their fill at the feast before the dancing began. When they took up their fiddles to play, the party got into full swing. The fiddlers played their hearts out but did so with great pleasure as the music was enlivening and uplifting and the dancing ladies were a joy to behold. Time passed, and they hardly seemed to notice it.

At last, when it seemed that morning had come, the dancing came to a halt and the fiddlers packed up, ready to leave. The old man who had hired them paid them generously with a bag of silver and the fiddlers departed from the hillock in fine spirits. It had been a great night and a most profitable one. They wandered back towards Inverness, and it was here that things seemed to take a strange turn. Everything was different. The town itself had changed so much that they hardly recognised it as the same place. New buildings had sprung up, as if from nowhere. The people had changed too. They all wore very different clothes and laughed when they saw what the fiddlers were wearing, calling their attire 'strange' and 'old-fashioned'.

The fiddlers could not work out what was wrong and decided to return to their own home town. Here they found that the situation was much the same. It was as if several tens of years had passed in the real world while the fiddlers had been away playing at the dance at Tomnahurich.

Finally, the two men tried to take refuge in religion and went to their local church. Their appearance caused quite a stir, but the congregation were silenced when the minister started to speak. Then, at the first mention of the name of God, the two fiddlers crumbled to dust in front of all those present.

The fact that the men were said to crumble to dust when the name of God was mentioned bears out another widespread belief about fairies – that their existence was somehow at odds with God and God's world; that they were, in fact, more associated with things demonic. Other stories about fairies often relate how the little creatures disappear at the mention of God.

Glaistigs

The glaistig was another supernatural being, a female who appeared in various forms and was sometimes associated with spirits of the dead. Some of the forms that this phenomenon was supposed to take on included half-woman, half-goat, a dog, a sheep, a woman in green and a monster. Whether or not the glaistig was a malevolent being is uncertain. Supernatural occurrences both catastrophic and benign have been attributed to glaistigs in different parts of Scotland at different times. Glaistigs have been commonly associated with water, said to live in places such as waterfalls, lochs and burns. Some were said to be particularly attached to, and protective of, animals, the young and the feeble, herding cows, playing games with children and caring for the sick and elderly. Some stories associate mischief with the concept of the glaistig, and activities similar to those of a poltergeist have been attributed to glaistigs in various folkloric tales. Other tales tell of much more sinister events, however, such as the waylaying and killing of travellers and the pronouncing of curses. Some people, accordingly, saw the glaistig as a manifestation of evil.

Where the glaistig came from or how she came into existence was also a matter of differing opinions, but the link with the dead was never far away. She was sometimes perceived as a human being who had fallen under fairy enchantment; sometimes she was seen as a spirit of a dead person, sometimes a devilish creature with malicious intent. Whatever she was, or wherever she came from, the glaistig was tied in with traditions that link the idea of an afterlife with that of some sort of realm coexistent with the world of the living but inhabited by supernatural beings.

Green Ladies

There are links between the concept of the glaistig and the many tales that are told of green-lady ghosts. Green ladies pop up here, there and everywhere in Scotland, and are often regular visitors and familiar sights to the people and the places that they haunt. Glaistigs, as has been already mentioned, were sometimes said to appear as ladies dressed in green.

Some green-lady ghosts have acquired a reputation for a certain amount of mischief. This links them with some traditional perceptions of the glaistig. In addition to this, certain green-lady ghosts have been said to be able to assume different forms, such as those of a dog or a horse, a feature held in common with glaistigs.

Glaistigs were anonymous creatures, but this is not always the case with green-lady ghosts. Their identities and the reasons for their presence are often known to those whom they haunt.

Wailing Washerwomen

The Banshee

The sight or sound of a woman lamenting and washing clothes has for centuries been associated with doom and death in various parts of Scotland.

One such washerwoman was the banshee, who could be seen by streams and rivers, singing mournful laments as she washed the clothes of one or more people who were about to meet with a violent death. The banshee, it was said, could be approached with caution. If a mortal managed to sneak up to a banshee unnoticed, he or she could then take hold of her and ask her who was to die. Some people believed that, once caught, the banshee would also grant three wishes.

It is said that a banshee was heard wailing in Glencoe shortly before the massacre of the MacDonalds by the Campbells. Some of the MacDonalds heard the noise and, realising that they were in peril, fled to the hills. This, so it has been said, is one of the reasons why the massacre, awful though it was, was not as bad as it might have been. Forty members of the clan perished, it is true, but given the facts that they were outnumbered by the Campbells and taken by surprise during the night, the numbers of the dead were not as great as might have been anticipated.

The Caoineag

The caoineag was another grim spirit who made her presence felt when death was close, but she was less accessible to humans than the banshee. Like the banshee, she was heard to mourn and lament at the edge of a river or stream, but the caoineag was not visible to the human eye. She could not be approached and no one could talk to her. Those who heard the sound of her mourning were said to be doomed to face death or great sorrow.

The third type of ghostly washerwoman was believed to be the spectre of a woman who had died in childbirth. It was widely believed that when a woman died in such a manner, all her clothes had to be washed at once. If this was not done, the woman, who had died before her time was due, would be condemned to wash and to wail in some sort of limbo until she reached her 'due time' on earth; that is, until a time was reached when it would have been more natural and appropriate for her to die.

Devilish Struggles

There was a certain fascination, verging on preoccupation, with the devil long ago in Scotland. If anything or anyone was particularly feared for any reason, the hand of the devil had to be in there somewhere. Thus it was that men like John Graham of Claverhouse, 'Bonnie Dundee', came to be associated with the black arts. He was greatly feared, and the actions he took against his enemies, in particular the Covenanters, earned him widespread hatred. Stories began to circulate that his work was more than human and that he was in some way devilishly inspired. The rumours grew wilder over time. He was said to have consorted with the devil, to have practised the black arts and to have struck a deal with the devil whereby he would become invincible in battle. As the fear and loathing of the man increased in intensity, so the stories about him became more fantastic. Sir Tam Dalyell, a contemporary and ally of Claverhouse, earned himself a similar reputation.

The devil could be a convenient excuse for getting rid of someone who was proving to be a particular nuisance. Many a woman met a terrible death in Scotland in the sixteenth century, condemned for witchcraft and satanic practices. Some of these women might have been guilty of certain unsavoury practices; some, undoubtedly, practised the black arts. Nevertheless, it cannot be denied that, as far as many of them were concerned, they had done nothing to deserve their fate. Sometimes it was the case that a woman simply knew too much for her own good – a superior intellect and an inquiring mind were often treated with suspicion and could be enough to inspire a witch-hunt. Some women were too gossipy, others kept themselves to themselves too much, and the remainder simply behaved in a way that somebody, somehow, found offensive.

Those who did practise the black arts, both women and men, were said to be well acquainted with the devil. Those who admitted to such knowledge, or were forced into admission of such knowledge, suffered greatly for it. Some survived the rumours, but their notoriety lived on after them. If the stories that are told about them are to be believed, the spirits of people like these almost always seem to return. So we hear of the ghost of Major Weir, who consorted with the devil and still haunts the Old Town in Edinburgh, and the ghost of Alexander Skene, riding in his coach across the lake every year on Hogmanay to meet with Auld Nick.

The devil made frequent visits to the land of the living, according to tradition. He prowled the world of mortals in various forms, haunting the virtuous, tormenting the indecisive and tempting away the impious. Whether he appeared as man, beast or monster, the devil could always be identified by his cloven feet.

The story of Beardie of Glamis Castle, related later, in Ghostly Castles, is one of the many legends that tells of a visit from the devil to mere mortals – with disastrous consequences for foolish Beardie.

Another story, which comes from Galloway, tells of a meeting in Glenluce between a proud Highlander and the devil. Plague was rampaging the countryside, sent by the devil himself, and the Highlander and his family were among the fortunate few who had not caught it. The Highlander had jokingly boasted that he owed his own survival to two things – first, the fine Highland blood that coursed through his body; secondly, the fine malt whisky that also ran through his veins in large quantities.

The devil had been annoyed that someone should have the effrontery to speak of the plague in such a light-hearted manner. He appeared in front of the Highlander one night as the bold man was making his way home from the local hostelry. The devil challenged the Highlander to answer for his cheek, but the Highlander, full of Dutch courage, was undaunted. He felt up to any challenge that was offered him. After some debate, the devil and the Highlander agreed that they would hold a wrestling contest. If the devil won, he would infect the Highlander with the plague. If the Highlander won, the devil would have to put the plague in a bag and give it to the Highlander to dispose of.

The devil was strong, but the Highlander was a wily fighter. They wrestled with each other for some time without a clear victor emerging, both claiming to have won the tussle. In order to settle the argument, they hit upon the idea of a piping contest. The devil rustled up some pipes for them to play and the contest began. The devil, taking his turn first, played a fine tune, but when the Highlander picked up the pipes and began to play, the devil soon realised that here was a man who could play the pipes like no other. The Highlander's music was powerful and moving. It made the devil laugh, dance and weep in turn. The devil could not fail to be impressed and readily admitted defeat. He collected the plague together, like a big black cloud in his hand, then he sealed it in a bag and gave it to the Highlander as promised.

The Highlander had gambled with the devil, a dangerous pastime if ever there was one. Now he was one of the fortunate few who won. He took the bag that the devil had given him to the abbot in Glenluce to see what could be done to get rid of the plague once and for all. It took all the powers of the monks in the abbey to subdue the dark spirits of the plague but at last they succeeded, and the dreadful disease was gone from Galloway.

So we know that the devil was a gambler. He liked a game of cards, and he enjoyed pitting his wits against mere mortals. He was also a rogue with a liking for a good party. In whatever guise he appears in story or verse, as man or beast, the most frequent things associated with his appearance are music, dancing and wild times. Those who did choose to dabble in the occult and practise witchcraft may have traded their eternal souls when they did so, but they probably thought it worthwhile for the earthly pleasures of taking part in wild bacchanalian rites. Moreover, these pleasures did not necessarily come to an end with death.

The ghost of Major Weir is said to haunt the West Bow in Edinburgh still. He was executed after confessing to witchcraft, but following his death, the sounds that were said to emanate from his house before it was ultimately demolished were not those of tortured wailing or lament – they were the sounds of wild merrymaking. His earthly demise may have been most unpleasant, but his ghost, it would seem, was still having quite a good time of it.

Robert Burns' famous narrative poem 'Tam o' Shanter' portrays the devil as:

> ——in shape o' beast
> A towsy tyke, black, grim and large.

Burns' devil plays the pipes with gusto as the scantily clad witches dance around him with wild abandon. Tam fears for his life, and indeed his soul, when he comes upon the scene and sees the witches cavorting with the spirits of unchristened children and criminals. But in spite of himself he feels drawn to the sight. The devil and his entourage are having fun!

Other stories of the devil and his encounters with mortals tell of the devil being outdone, not so much by piety or the power of God as by sheer ingenuity. One particular legend that has been told of such a battle of wits between a mortal and the devil has been associated in slightly different versions with Michael Scott, the notorious thirteenth-century philosopher (some would say sorcerer), Lord Reay and another anonymous man. The stories differ only in detail; the essence is the same.

The devil has had encounters with the hero of the story before and is looking for a way to torment him. He gives the hero the use of one of his demonic servants to work for him at whichever tasks the hero chooses. The demonic worker is then set a variety of enormous tasks to carry out (bridge-building, barn-building, etc) and completes each task in record time, returning again and again for more work and giving the hero no peace. The hero finally hits upon a plan and instructs his tormentor to go down to the beach and construct a rope of sand. The demonic worker is then condemned to work forever at this impossible task. No sooner has something resembling a rope been made than the tide comes in and washes it away. The devil has been defeated once again.

The fear of the devil amongst the Scots, therefore, can be seen to have been counterbalanced by a certain amount of humour, and also, perhaps, a little envy. Nor is it always the case that those who have associated with the Evil One in life are seen to suffer for it after death. Ghosts with demonic associations are not necessarily unhappy ghosts, it would appear.

The Demon Crab

The devil appeared as many things. People saw him in the form of animals and strange monsters as well as in human form. Whenever something mysterious or sinister happened, signs of the devil were sought in case the events might be his work. One particular tale from Dundee illustrates quite well that no matter how ready mere mortals were to see Auld Nick, they were not always right in what they saw.

A tragedy had occurred – a brave ferryman had been caught with his boat in a squall and the boat had gone down with all its passengers. Some time later, when the storm had finally subsided, the body of the ferryman was washed up ashore, just in front of the cottage where he had lived. The body was pulled into the cottage and laid out carefully in order that the locals might come and pay their respects. There was quite a crowd gathered. They stood in respectful silence as they looked at the bedraggled corpse of the drowned man.

Suddenly, someone saw a movement in the sleeve of the dead man's jacket. The crowd gave a gasp – the corpse was stirring! The corpse, however, lay quite still, and out of the sleeve crawled an enormous black crab. To the superstitious fisherfolk present, the crab could be only one thing – the devil himself! Everyone jumped back as the satanic beast scuttled across the floor of the cottage and made for the door. A path was quickly cleared to let the crab move on towards the sea – no one dared impede the progress of the devil!

At that moment an elderly fishwife stepped forward, scooped up the crab and tucked it securely in her pinny. Much to everyone's horror, she announced that it was a meal too good to waste. Stories flew here and there for many days afterwards about the terrible smells that issued from the fishwife's cottage as she cooked the crab. Some people even claimed to have seen a beastly black form flying out of the cottage as the fishwife put the crab in the pot to boil. In spite of the conjectures and rumours, however, no one could deny the fact that the fishwife ate the crab, enjoyed it, and came to no harm from the experience. People might have been reluctant to admit it, but it seemed that they had got it wrong about the Demon Crab.

DEATH AND DYING: GHOSTLY HORDES AND PHANTOM LIGHTS

Many superstitions survive to this day concerning the dead and the dying in Scotland. They have their origins in times when people were much more familiar with death, particularly premature death, than they are nowadays, when the country is no longer torn by war and internal feuding and when medical science is able to ensure that most of us at least survive into old age.

The custom of sitting up with a corpse before the funeral – the wake, or lykewake – has its origins in the belief that the body of the dead person needed protection from unwanted spiritual inter-ference before it was given a proper burial. In the past there were several symbolic rites associated with the wake, intended to protect the spirit of the dead and send it safely to the afterlife, and also to protect those who remained living.

Those who sat up with the body at night were provided with a bible, a candle, whisky and food. In some parts of the country it was tradition that there was to be no fire lit in the room in which the corpse lay. The spirit of the dead person was in danger of being interfered with by the forces of evil and therefore no chances were taken with the corpse awaiting burial. Domestic animals were kept well away; if a cat or a dog passed over the body it had to be killed. Mirrors in the room were covered up, and if there was a clock in the room, it had to be stopped.

Those who sat up at night with the corpse had to remain there until daylight. If they left in the dark, it was believed that they might witness something fearful.

When the corpse had been laid out, a wooden platter was placed on its chest. On the platter was placed a small pile of earth –

symbolic of the body – and another of salt – the spirit, which lived on after death. Sometimes only a small pile of salt was placed on the body.

In spite of all the precautions that were taken to ensure the safety of the dead person's spirit and the souls of those who had come to keep the corpse company, the lykewake was not always mournful by any means. It could be quite a social occasion. In some parts, the long night was whiled away with storytelling and singing – even dancing was not unknown.

Signs of Death

Signs of approaching death were many. Individual stories of people who have witnessed some of these signs are told in another chapter, 'Signs, Prophecies and Curses' (see page 163). The gift (or curse) of second sight has often revealed itself for the first (sometimes the only) time when somebody has seen, or dreamt, of an imminent death. Many other stories record ghostly happenings or sights that then turn out to have been warnings of death. Some of these occurrences are very individual in nature, but there are others that have come to be accepted widely as death warnings, communications from the realm of the dead to the land of the living through a living medium.

Death Lights

Sightings of death lights, or death candles as they were often known, were quite commonly reported. These were lights that were seen in graveyards, close to the sickbed of a dying person or near the site of an imminent death or disaster. Thus an unfamiliar light seen on water was believed to foretell a drowning or a tragedy at sea, and a light above a house meant that death would take place therein before long.

Ghostly lights, similar to death lights, have often been reported shining at the sites of tragedies, in particular ancient battlefields. Rather than warnings of death to come, these lights seem to be markers or reminders of death that has gone before.

Ghosts of the Living

A ghostly figure of a person still alive might be seen alongside that person or sometimes in another place. This was taken to be an ominous sign. Death was not far away.

Phantom Funerals

Phantom funerals, causing surprise and distress to those who witnessed them, were relatively common supernatural occurrences. Sometimes reports of such funerals record the witness as having merely seen and heard such a ghostly procession. However, there are stories of people who have been pushed aside in the roadway as the phantom mourners make their way past. To witness such an event was never a good sign.

One story of a phantom funeral comes from the fishing town of Wick in the north of Scotland. The story tells how a crofter from Wick was visited every year by his cousin, who was a fisherman and came to the port for the herring run. While his fishing boat was based at Wick, he would spend his spare time at the crofter's house. The two men got along famously in spite of their different lifestyles.

One particular year, the fisherman was preparing to set sail for home after a successful season with the herring fishing. His cousin, although not a fisherman, still had a healthy respect for the sea and his farming experience had given him a keen eye for the weather. He felt that the weather was about to take a turn for the worse and urged the fisherman to stay a little longer in Wick. His time there had shown him a healthy profit – what was the hurry?

The fisherman brushed aside the concerns of his cousin and laughed off any suggestion that the weather was too dangerous to go to sea. He was an experienced seaman and his boat was sturdy enough to withstand any squall. He bade goodbye to his crofter cousin and set off.

During the day, the weather turned worse, just as the crofter had suspected it would. The crofter had spent the afternoon visiting a family some way from his own home and when he saw the skies darken, he decided he had better make his way back.

The weather turned very wild with alarming speed and a fierce storm was blowing as the crofter trudged home, battling against the gale. He was halfway home when he saw a strange sight – three men carrying a coffin in the direction of the graveyard.

It seemed a small number of people for a funeral procession – perhaps the bad weather was keeping the mourners away. Curiosity overcame the crofter, and he followed the sombre procession to the cemetery. The three men stopped and put the coffin on the ground for a moment or two. Approaching the silent group, the crofter leaned over the coffin for a closer look. He could just make out the name that was engraved on the brass plate on top. It was his cousin's name. The crofter then looked up at the three coffin-bearers. Their faces were all too grimly familiar – they were the faces of three other men from Wick who had been lost at sea within the last year.

The crofter made for home with dread in his heart. When the news reached him some days later that his cousin had drowned after falling overboard in the storm, he was not surprised at all. He had already learnt of his cousin's fate, the night when he had seen the phantom funeral.

Canine Sense

Dogs are still widely believed to be able to see what many human beings cannot. They are thought to be sensitive to supernatural presences and will often show signs of fear and distress before any human being has realised that anything is amiss. Dogs can sense the presence of ghosts. In times gone by, a dog howling in the night for no other apparent reason would often be taken as a sign of approaching death. Some people believed that a dog howling like this should be able to indicate, by pointing, the direction in which the death would take place.

Birds

Birds, both domestic and wild, were believed be 'tuned in' to the world of the supernatural and were said to be able to foretell death. Poultry were observed with apprehension in some places in Scotland. A cockerel crowing uncharacteristically in the hours of darkness was thought to mean the approach of death somewhere in the vicinity. Hens showing signs of fear and panic in spite of the absence of any predator in the vicinity were often believed to be foretelling doom for someone close by.

If a raven flew in front of someone along the road that he or she was taking, it was believed to be a bad sign – death was not far away for that person. Birds tapping on the window of a house were an equally unfortunate sign, as was a seagull standing on one leg on the roof of a house.

Death in Foreign Lands

> *'Oh, ye'll tak the High Road, and I'll tak the Low Road*
> *And I'll be in Scotland before ye;*
> *For me and my true love will never meet again*
> *On the bonnie, bonnie banks of Loch Lomond.'*

The lines above, the chorus of a song nowadays more often sung raucously (or drunkenly) than mournfully, reflect another belief about the spirits of the dead. The song is thought to have been written around the time of the Rebellion of the '45. In 1745, some supporters of Bonnie Prince Charlie, retreating from England, were captured by the English. The words of the song are the words of one soldier who faces execution to another who is to be freed. The soldier who is about to die tells his friend that he will take the 'Low Road' back to Scotland. The Low Road was the name of a spiritual path that was believed to exist along which the spirits of those who died far from home could return to the place of their birth. The Low Road would speed the executed soldier to Scotland faster than his compatriot, who faced many miles of hard marching, but although he might return to his homeland swiftly enough after death, he would never meet with his sweetheart again.

Phantom Hordes

The dead were never far away. Whatever happened to their bodies, the spirits of those who had died had to go somewhere. Whilst some spiritual presences were believed to be benign, inevitably there were many fears about spirits of the dead who wished harm upon the living. Superstition about such malevolent forces was prevalent throughout Scotland.

The realm of the dead was seen in much the same way as the realm of the fairies. Living persons could be spirited away to either realm, either temporarily or permanently. Those who claimed to have gone through such an experience were usually greatly changed by it. In common with stories of visits to the fairy realm, tales of being spirited away by the dead indicated that time in the realm of the dead was different from earthly time. Great distances were travelled in no time at all, and although several hours, or even days, might seem to pass, the person who had been spirited away, once safely back in the land of mortals, would discover that his or her absence had been very brief in earthly time.

The Sluagh, or host of the dead, was greatly feared in the Highlands. The sight and sound of their grim parades through the realms of the living struck terror into the hearts of those who witnessed them. The Sluagh could bring death to those in its path. Those of a superstitious nature would not leave a window on the west side of the house open at night. To do so was to court disaster, for the Sluagh could then enter and cause trouble.

POLTERGEISTS

Poltergeists are a well-documented phenomenon world-wide. Whether or not they are ghosts as such is a matter of some debate. They are not generally associated with any particular person who has gone into the hereafter. Their activities are generally short-lived, the hauntings of a poltergeist not going on indefinitely. Instead, there is generally a period of some weeks or months when activity is particularly troublesome. After this time, the poltergeist will disappear or at least cease its activities.

Poltergeists are closely associated with adolescents, especially troubled children. The appearance of a poltergeist will often coincide with a time of particular trauma for a teenager in the household, whether the trouble be of a serious nature or the usual adolescent angst.

There have been many reported incidents of poltergeist activity throughout Scotland.

Andrew Mackie's House

Perhaps the most famous poltergeist is that which came to haunt the house of Andrew Mackie, a farmer in Ringcroft of Stocking, Kirkcudbrightshire. This story is particularly unusual because it was documented in great detail at the time by a local minister who was very much involved in the whole affair, the Reverend Andrew Telfair. His report is backed up by the testimony of several witnesses, amongst whom are other members of the clergy.

The story dates back three hundred years to the end of the seventeenth century when, inexplicably, the family of Andrew Mackie began to be tormented by some sort of devilish spirit. The haunting lasted for a period of some three months.

The strange events began one night in February 1695, when Andrew Mackie went out to check on his cattle. When he got to the byre, he found all the beasts running loose. A little puzzled, he tied them up carefully before retiring for the night. Next morning, however, when he went to attend to them, he found that they had become untethered once more. The next night, the same thing happened again. Andrew tied his beasts with even extra care, only to find them let loose, how he knew not, by the next morning. The next morning again he found one of his cattle suspended from the roof of the cow shed by its tether.

The odd happenings in the cow shed then began to be followed up by disturbances in the house. One night, a basket full of peat that had been standing outside found its way into the house as the family slept. The basket was upturned, and the peat was piled up in a heap in the middle of the house. Somehow, the peat had been set alight. Fortunately the family was wakened by the smell of smoke and disaster was averted.

There then followed a period in the month of March when the house was bombarded by stones. The stones came from no one knew where; no one seemed to be throwing them. At first, the odd small stone was seen to fly through the air outside the house. Gradually, the stones increased in size and number, hurled by some unseen force around the house, hitting the building and its occupants.

The disturbances continued – kitchen implements, furniture and bedding were inexplicably moved, turning up in the strangest of places. On one occasion a child of the family was alarmed to see a figure huddled in his blanket in the corner of the room, close to the fire. When someone had plucked up the courage to investigate and pulled the blanket back, it was found that it was not a person under the cover but an upturned stool.

The flying stones became bigger and better in their aim; the members of the family were being knocked and bruised by them and neighbours coming to call were similarly assaulted.

The house was continually disrupted by bangs, knockings, furniture moving and doors slamming. Over time, the family observed that the activities of this strange spirit, if spirit it was, were more frantic on Sundays or at times when the members of the family were praying together.

As the trouble escalated, the family called in Reverend Telfair. He led the family in prayers, but as soon as he left the house, the stone-throwing resumed. Things calmed down in the following few days, but the next Sabbath saw an increase in the stone-throwing. Reverend Telfair offered to spend the night with the family. The spirit rewarded his efforts with more frantic activity. Telfair himself was struck by stones and a stick. Furniture made strange noises; objects flew at people across the room.

As Telfair knelt in prayer, he felt something on his arm and looking down, saw a ghostly white hand at his wrist.

In the following days, the spirit continued to vent its anger. People were hurled across rooms in the house, scratched, had their hair pulled and were beaten with sticks. The stone-throwing continued relentlessly. The children had their covers torn off them as they lay in their beds. Then they were beaten about the hips by an invisible hand.

The spirit began to make itself heard. As the family were praying, they heard a voice saying, 'Whist! Whist!'

The torment continued unabated until April, and the bravery and tenacity of the family must have been considerable, for they remained in the house in spite of it all. In April, Telfair sought the assistance of his fellow clergy, and two ministers, Andrew Ewart and John Murdo, from Kells and Crossmichael respectively, joined the Mackie family in prayer one night. The ministers suffered considerable pains for their efforts; huge stones were flung at them both and they were beaten with sticks. The whole house was in more turmoil than ever. Fires began to break out.

One day, Andrew Mackie's wife was stepping into the yard when she noticed that a stone slab in the doorway was loose. She lifted the slab and found some bones and bloody flesh underneath, wrapped in cloth. She took the bones from the house to the landlord's house, quite some distance away, thinking that the trouble might in some way be associated with the bones. In her absence, the trouble in the house only increased. The children found burning hot stones in their beds. Fireballs flew around. The stone-throwing was worse than ever. Mrs Mackie returned the bones to the house. The Reverend Telfair prayed over the bones and was beaten severely with a stick.

And so it went on. Then something happened that made all concerned wonder whether there was something in the house's past to cause the spiritual disturbances. One day, Andrew Mackie found a note, written in blood, or so it appeared, close to his house.

'3 Years thou shall have to repent a nett it well,' the note read. 'Wo be to thee Scotland Repent and tak warning for the doors of haven ar all Redy bart against thee, I am sent for a warning to thee to flee to God yet troublt shall this man be for twenty days repent repent repent Scotland or else thou shall.'

Was there a connection between the bones and the message? Had there been a murder in the house? The house was not old; it had been built only twenty-eight years before. An investigation into the past history of the building ought not to be difficult. Accordingly, all previous occupants were brought before a committee consisting of Andrew Telfair, the landlord, Charles Maclellan, and others. They were all asked to touch the bones. Nothing untoward occurred, so the committee sent the bones to Kirkcudbright for examination by an assembly of ministers. Five ministers were then dispatched to Andrew Mackie's house to pray. The spirit, angered as ever by religious intrusion, flew into a fury. Stones broke through the roof of the house, and the whole building seemed to shake. Telfair details some of the spirit's activities as follows:

It brake down the barne door and mid-wall and threw stones up the house; But it did no great hurt: it gripped, and handled the legs of some, as with a man's hand; it hoisted up the feet of others while standing on the ground, thus it did to William Lennox of Mill-House, my self and others, in this manner it continued till ten a clock at night.

The ministers persisted for three days, but the spirit would not give in to their prayers. Other people from the district joined in the effort. At one point a neighbour appeared with his dog. The dog had killed a polecat on the way to the Mackie's house and the visitor threw the dead creature in a corner of the room before joining in the prayers. Three more people arrived and were very distressed when the spirit picked up the dead animal and beat them about the heads and bodies with its carcass. One of the visitors felt something like a hand inside his clothes and pockets and became so distraught that he was sick.

The following Sabbath brought even more upset. The spirit whispered and whistled and cried out at the family in prayer. The family and friends and neighbours were injured with stones and sticks. Praying men were lifted off their knees by the unseen force.

Two days later, on 16 April, the Mackie family had had enough. They decided to move out of the house for a while. Five of their neighbours volunteered to stay in the house in the Mackies' absence. Strangely, the trouble in the house stopped and the guests were not bothered by the spirit at all. Outside, however, the cattle were found to have broken loose from their tethers, and some appeared to have been disturbed.

Thinking that things might be improving, some members of the family moved back in after a couple of days. They spent one peaceful night, but in the morning found that the sheep had been tied together in pairs by tethers fashioned from straw that had been taken from the stable. After two reasonably quiet days, the spirit started again, with a vengeance. The beating and stone-throwing began again, and lumps of peat were thrown along with the stones. The spirit whistled and called out, 'Take you that!' as it beat its victims. All present continued with their prayers, but the harder they prayed, the more they suffered.

Andrew Mackie was snatching a few hours of sleep when he was woken by the voice of the spirit: 'Thou shalt be troubled till Tuesday,' it said.

Mackie decided to try to talk to the spirit.

'Who gave thee a commission?' he asked.

'God gave me a commission,' was the reply, 'and I am sent to warn the land to repent, for a judgement is to come if the land do not quickly repent and I will return a hundred times worse upon every family in the land. Praise me and I will whistle to you; worship me and I will trouble you no more.'

Mackie prayed for deliverance from Satan. The spirit's reaction was contemptuous: 'You might as well have said Shadrach, Meshach and Abednego.'

Several people heard the conversation between Andrew Mackie and the spirit. One of the company attempted to intervene, but the spirit would not countenance this, dismissing the man for meddling in other people's business. When the spirit became silent once more, the family was no further forward.

The next day, there were seven fires around the house started by the spirit, and the family and neighbours were kept hard at work all day extinguishing them. The spirit appeared to be frustrated at the success of their efforts and began to tear down one of the house walls. The family was forced to take refuge in a barn. As they tried to get some rest, the spirit raised a great block of wood in the air above the heads of the children. 'If I had a commission I would brain them!' it cried angrily.

The fire-raising and the exhausting task of keeping the fires under control continued all the following day. Mackie was in the barn when the spirit spoke to him again.

'Andrew. Andrew.'

Mackie tried to ignore the voice.

'Speak!' commanded the spirit.

Andrew would not speak.

The spirit spoke again, in a calmer tone: 'Be not troubled. You shall have no more trouble, except some casting of stones upon Tuesday to fulfil the promise.'

Telfair, Maclellan and some others joined the family late that night in the house and stayed there for some hours. Apart from some stone-throwing, all was quiet.

On Tuesday, the day upon which the spirit had said it would stop its troubles, the Mackie family and others gathered in the barn to pray. Mackie was the first to catch sight of a black thing in the corner of the building. The thing grew, and it seemed as if it might fill the whole barn with its presence. It was like a huge, black storm cloud. Chaff and mud flew out of the cloud at the terrified onlookers, who then felt themselves being gripped painfully hard around the arms and bodies by the blackness itself. Then the blackness subsided. Everything returned to normal. A quiet night followed.

On the last Wednesday, 1 May, there was one final fire. A sheep house was destroyed, but neither people nor animals were hurt in any way. The disturbances at Ringcroft of Stocking were finally over, and no one was the wiser as to what had caused them.

There were some theories as to what might have triggered the trouble. Reverend Telfair put three of these forward in his account of the happenings.

Some years before the house was occupied by the Mackie family, it was the home of a man called McNaught. McNaught was a miserable soul. Desperately poor and in frail health, he wondered if some evil force might have taken ill against him. He had sent his son to ask the advice of a spae-wife, or fortune-teller, some distance away. His son had gone to see the woman but had met some soldiers on his way home, enlisted and gone abroad. He finally sent a message back to Ringcroft relating the spae-wife's advice. Under a slab at the threshold of the house could be found a tooth. When the tooth was removed and burnt, good fortune would return to the house. The message got back to Ringcroft too late, however, for Mr McNaught was dead.

The new tenant of the house, a man called Thomas Telfair (no relation of Reverend Telfair), heard of the spae-wife's words, lifted the stone, found a tooth and burned it. He had had no trouble whilst in the house. Perhaps McNaught's misery, Telfair's trouble-free tenancy and Andrew Mackie's troubles were somehow linked.

A second theory concerned the death of a woman of ill-repute whose belongings had been left in the house after she died. Perhaps the Mackies had taken the things for themselves? Mackie denied this strongly, saying that the woman's things, carefully tied in a bundle, had been returned to her nearest and dearest intact.

The third theory was dismissed outright by Telfair, who knew Andrew Mackie to be a good, God-fearing citizen. The theory was that Mackie, when he became a mason, had dedicated his first child to the devil.

The strange occurrences have sparked off many a lively debate in the years that have followed, but no one has come any closer to finding out what it was that tormented the family of Andrew Mackie for three terrible months in 1695. Why it caused so much trouble is just as much of a mystery and will no doubt remain so.

The Devil of Glenluce

Forty years before the astonishing catalogue of events at Ringcroft of Stocking, the household of Gilbert Campbell, a weaver in Glenluce, was disrupted by a similar presence. This story is more typical of poltergeist activity than that of Andrew Mackie's house, in that the spirit appeared to be closely connected to the children in the family, in particular to Campbell's son, a young student at Glasgow University.

The first indication of trouble to come was given when Campbell's daughter, Jennet, began to complain of strange noises in her ears. The noises were shrill, like whistling. Then Jennet was heard to utter the words of some unseen spirit: 'I'll cast thee, Jennet, into the well.'

After that, the house was subjected to continual bombardment with stones. Clothing was hurled from drawers, clothes were ripped to shreds, sleepers were woken as the bedclothes were dragged off them by an invisible force.

Much alarmed, Campbell moved his children out of the house for their own safety. The disturbances ceased as soon as the children had gone. The children moved back into the house with the exception of the eldest son, who was studying in Glasgow. For a while things were quiet, but then Campbell's son returned to the house and the trouble started again with renewed vigour. Stones were hurled around, belongings were damaged, and at one point the house caught fire.

The affair caught the attention of the church, and various attempts were made by ministers to exorcise the spirit. The spirit was apparently quite communicative and claimed to have Campbell's son in its power. It claimed to have been sent by Satan from hell to torment the occupants of the house.

While the spirit was willing to communicate with the religious men, it was nevertheless resistant to all their attempts to banish it from the house. It continued to torment the family, beating the children as they lay in their beds, starting fires around the house, hiding the family's belongings or hurling them through the air.

The family showed remarkable courage, remaining in the house throughout all this. Then, without warning, the activities of the malevolent force stopped, and the family was left in peace.

Although no one could be certain as to the cause of the fearful disturbances, one theory connects them to a beggar who had turned up at Campbell's house some time previously. Campbell had sent him away without giving him a penny, and the beggar had angrily threatened to avenge this cold-hearted treatment. It was said that the man was a certain Alexander Agnew, who was eventually accused of crimes against the church and was hanged some miles away in Dumfries. His death apparently coincided with the sudden return to harmony at Campbell's house in Glenluce.

The Poltergeist of Sauchie

A much more recent case of poltergeist activity was that which concerned a young girl called Virginia Campbell who lived in the village of Sauchie in Clackmannanshire. The story caused quite a sensation in 1960–61.

The child had moved to Scotland from Ireland with her parents, and by all appearances was a normal, bright little girl. The move to

37

Scotland might have been more traumatic for Virginia than people around her had realised. Perhaps this, along with the fact that she was at a vulnerable age – she was eleven at the time – accounted for the strange occurrences that took place when she was around.

The strange events started in the child's home. Unexplained knocking noises were heard when she was around, and objects, even surprisingly heavy ones, were seen to move. The child herself was very distressed by what was happening. Her mother kept her home from school and called the doctor, who prescribed tranquillisers. Virginia seemed calmer, but the strange things went on happening. The doctor had some idea that what they were witnessing might be poltergeist activity. In order to try to eliminate this possibility, Virginia was sent to stay the night with relatives, but the strange events went with her. She was clearly the focus of some sort of paranormal activity. After a couple of weeks, things began to calm down, and it was decided that she should return to school.

Virginia's mother told teachers at the school that odd things were happening at home. Objects were moving; some were flying through the air. It all seemed too strange to be true, but initial scepticism on the part of the teachers soon disappeared when similar things began to happen around Virginia at school. Her desk rose inches from the floor. Other children in her class noticed objects moving from place to place. Once, a door refused to shut behind her. Heavy furniture could be seen to move. Although the activities were less violent in nature than had been witnessed in Virginia's home, they were still happening.

Over the next few months, it became more and more difficult to safeguard the child from the morbid interest of the press. The stories that were circulated were sometimes only tenuously linked to the facts. Surprisingly, the other children in the school were much less hysterical than outsiders in their reactions to events. They became quite matter-of-fact about the situation; when Virginia was around, sometimes things moved – simple as that.

The strange happenings became less and less frequent over time, and after a few months they had stopped altogether.

A HAUNTED CAPITAL

Edinburgh is a beautiful city, of that there can be no doubt. Dubbed the 'Athens of the North' because of the number of classical style buildings it boasts in its graceful Georgian New Town, it also has a proud and ancient castle and a stunning palace that is still a royal residence. Clustered round the Royal Mile, the street that stretches downhill west to east from Edinburgh Castle to the Palace of Holyroodhouse, are the remains of the Old Town, higgledy-piggledy tenements and closes, along with the Canongate, the Grassmarket and the West Bow, all steeped in history and, so we are told, heavily populated by ghostly presences. Edinburgh has seen it all in its time – conflict and siege, plague and fire, murder, intrigue and witchcraft. Seedy and gruesome characters from the past provide a wealth of great material for tourist guides. It must be a joy to have stories about body-snatchers, witch trials and particularly cruel executions to relate to your audience as you stroll the streets of the city with a crowd of visitors. There is enough to tell based on historical fact alone to keep an audience spellbound, but wise tourist guides will know their ghosts as well. There are plenty of them, after all, and their stories add to the thrill of the place. Visitors to Edinburgh can now choose to scare themselves silly on guided tours that specifically concentrate on the horrors of the past and the ghouls that are said to lurk in their wake.

Ghosts can make good money for the entrepreneur, but their manifestations were first recorded long before ghost tours were even thought of, and some of the stories have been passed down through several generations. How did the stories start? Do the ghosts exist? It is left to the individual to decide, for neither the sceptic nor the believer can prove to each other unequivocally whether or not the ghosts do exist.

Edinburgh's ghosts are not all ancient. Things continue to

happen in places in and around the town that cannot be explained. The catalogue of reports of supernatural phenomena continues to grow. What is it all about? Is it all hysteria, sensationalism, superstitious nonsense? Is there a rational explanation for everything? The debate will probably never reach a conclusion. Meanwhile, stories of Edinburgh's ghosts will continue to keep children from sleeping soundly and make people stop in their tracks on dark nights in dim cobbled streets – is there anybody there?

Ann Street – The Return of Mr Swan

Ann Street is a particularly beautiful and desirable place to live in the heart of Georgian Edinburgh. At the end of the nineteenth century, one of the houses in the street was home to the Swan family. An uncle of the family was a great traveller, and the family was used to receiving letters from far-flung places describing his latest exploits. The traveller would take off for months at a time but would always keep in touch by mail and would appear from time to time, sometimes without warning, to draw breath between his adventures.

One evening the family was particularly surprised to see Mr Swan appear in their midst. They had expected him to be far away at sea, but they were delighted all the same. They rose to greet him as he strolled in through the front door, but before they had time to make him welcome, Mr Swan merely smiled at them, waved and disappeared. It was the oddest thing. The family was left to ponder the strange occurrence for some weeks until news finally reached them that Mr Swan had drowned when the ship in which he had been travelling to some distant place had sunk. The time of his death coincided with his mysterious appearance in the family home. His 'visit' had apparently been a wish to keep in touch with his nearest and dearest in death just as he had in life.

Mr Swan still returns to his old family home in Ann Street. Far from being a malevolent figure, it is said that he is very much a friendly ghost, popping in to say hello.

Charlotte Square – A Ghostly Piano

Charlotte Square in the west end of the city is a busy place and is for the most part taken up with offices. But in amongst the hustle and bustle of city life, through the continual noise of the passing traffic, another sound can sometimes be heard – that of ghostly piano playing.

Corstorphine – The Haunted Sycamore Tree

Nothing remains of Corstorphine Castle apart from the ancient dovecot that stands near the east end of Dovecot Road in Corstorphine, a suburb on the northwest side of Edinburgh. The castle was destroyed in the eighteenth century. Beside the dovecot once stood an old, gnarled sycamore tree, the last of an avenue of trees that led westwards towards the castle. The tree, diseased and fragile, was carefully preserved as a well-loved historical landmark by the Corstorphine Trust until it finally gave way during a storm on the night of 26 December, 1998. The trunk snapped in two leaving nothing standing but a jagged stump.

The story of the Corstorphine sycamore and the White Lady who haunts it, is familiar to all in the district, young and old alike.

In the seventeenth century, when the castle of Corstorphine was still standing, it was inhabited by the Forrester family, who owned most of the land in the surrounding area. The laird at the time, one James Forrester, was a charismatic man, whose overindulgence in alcohol and whose liking for a pretty face and curving figure were well known but, on the whole, forgiven on account of his great charm.

Laird James became embroiled in a passionate affair with a married woman, Christian Nimmo. The lovers were forced to meet in secret, which must have added both a great deal of excitement and a certain amount of tension to the liaison. One such meeting, in the shadows of the dovecot beside the sycamore tree, was destined

41

to be their final. It began with a passionate embrace and ended in a murder.

When Christian Nimmo arrived at their appointed meeting place, Sir James was not there, but Christian knew his habits all too well and sent one of her servants to the Black Bull Inn nearby to seek him out. The laird was found in the inn, as anticipated, and he finally came to meet her by the sycamore tree. He had been drinking heavily, and Christian Nimmo, angered by his inconsiderate and objectionable behaviour, began to quarrel with him. The dispute swiftly took on frightening proportions until suddenly, seized by a fit of uncontrollable rage, the lady pulled her lover's sword from its scabbard by his side and plunged it into him. She escaped from justice initially but was eventually hunted down and taken to meet her end at the hands of the executioner. Her ghost, dressed all in white, haunts the area around the dovecot still, the bloody sword in her hand giving evidence of the dreadful consequences of her temper.

Dalry – The One-Armed Ghost of John Chiesly

This ghostly figure was known as 'Johnny One-Arm' to the people around Dalry in Edinburgh. He haunted the streets of the area, scaring grown-ups and children alike, for more than three hundred years.

John Chiesly lived in the middle of the sixteenth century, an unhappily married man until he finally sought a divorce from his wife in 1688. He then became an unhappily divorced man. The Lord President of the Court of Session, Sir George Lockhart, had pronounced that John Chiesly should pay his wife a substantial sum annually in settlement. Feeling the sum awarded to be entirely unreasonable, being out of all proportion both to his wife's needs and his own means, John Chiesly decided to vent his anger upon Sir George. He followed him to church one Sunday morning and, catching up with him in Old Bank Close, he shot him. Sir George died, and the full weight of the law descended upon John Chiesly.

He was tortured cruelly to establish whether he had acted alone or with the help of others. Then his right arm was cut off while he was still alive as fitting punishment for its part in the crime – his right hand had held the murder weapon. Finally, John Chiesly was taken to the gallows and hanged. His body was left hanging on the gallows as an example and a gruesome warning to all. Then someone – nobody knew who – took the body down and secreted it away. Had it been buried? Nobody could, or would, tell.

Ghostly happenings began to be reported in Dalry. Several people reported seeing the anguished figure of a man in the streets around the area. The ghost had one arm missing. It screamed. It laughed maniacally. It gave the neighbouring children nightmares. The ghost appeared, again and again, over the next three hundred years.

In 1965, builders started work in a cottage in Dalry. On removing part of the floor they were surprised to find the skeleton of a man. The skeleton was cracked and broken, as one would expect the skeleton of a tortured man to be. Most significantly, however, the skeleton had only one hand. It could only be John Chiesly. The remains were removed from the house and re-interred in another place. The streets of Dalry are at peace now, for Johnny One-Arm no longer has cause to haunt them.

Edinburgh Castle – Phantom Musicians

Edinburgh Castle has seen more than its fair share of drama and tragedy over the centuries. No doubt there are more ghostly tales to be told about the fortress that stands so proudly on the rock above the city, but the two most famous stories concern a phantom piper and a (sometimes headless) drummer. Both are fitting tales to tell about Edinburgh Castle – the sound of pipes and drums is inextricably linked with the castle in modern times, for it is the venue of the world-famous Edinburgh Military Tattoo, in which massed bands from regiments all over the world thrill audiences of several hundred a night for three weeks every year.

The Phantom Piper

Edinburgh Castle has seen many alterations and additions since it first came into being as a fortified stronghold. The oldest surviving building on Castle Rock is St Margaret's Chapel, built in the twelfth century, but over the following centuries walls, ramparts, vaults, batteries and a cluster of buildings with both grand and prosaic functions were added until the whole finally came to resemble the castle as people can see it today, complete with a modern visitor centre.

The story goes that in the course of some of these building works (although no one seems sure of when or for what purpose), workmen came upon the entrance to a tunnel that appeared to be leading down through Castle Rock, underneath the Royal Mile. In order to establish how long the tunnel was and where it went, a piper was dispatched to walk as far as he could, playing his pipes as he went, thereby allowing those who remained above ground to follow the sounds of his music and trace the tunnel's route.

It seemed like a good plan at the time. The piper set off, and the people above waited and listened. The sound of playing bagpipes could be heard, albeit faintly, and the sound was moving down the Royal Mile, much as everybody had expected it would. The people above ground kept listening and following the sound. Suddenly, getting towards halfway down the Royal Mile, the piping stopped. There seems to be no record of anybody having gone to look for the hapless piper; perhaps they were all too scared. Rather than take the investigations any further, it was decided to seal the tunnel once more and forget all about it. To this day, it is said, if you listen hard enough above the sounds of the traffic on the stretch of the Royal Mile that leads from Edinburgh Castle to South Bridge, you might just hear the sound of subterranean bagpipe music, for the ghost of the piper still plays in the tunnel below the street.

The phantom piper at Edinburgh Castle is not unique. Elsewhere in Scotland, according to legend, the sound of ghostly bagpipes can be heard in more than one other place, hidden below the earth. See 'Ghostly Castles – Gight Castle' (page 70).

The Ghostly Drummer

The story of the drummer at Edinburgh Castle appears to date from the middle of the seventeenth century. Soldiers were garrisoned at the castle under the command of the governor at the time, Colonel Walter Dundas. One night the sentry on guard duty was startled by the sound of a military drum being played. On looking up, he saw a drummer marching on the battlements, beating out a warning of impending attack. The sentry fired his musket and raised the alarm. When others came to his aid, nothing could be seen or heard of the drummer, and the sentry was locked up, suspected of being under the influence of drink while on duty. On subsequent nights, however, the drummer was seen again by different sentries and was heard playing his drum by the governor of the Castle himself. The drummer was obviously a spectre of some sort, but no one knew why the figure kept appearing.

Perhaps the drummer was trying to tell the occupants of the Castle something. Later that year, when the Castle was besieged by Cromwell's troops, the appearance of the ghostly drummer was perceived, with hindsight, to have been a warning of such an occurrence. To this day, there are claims that the drummer still appears from time to time, disturbing the peace of the night with the noise of his drumbeat. Some say the drummer is headless.

George Street – The Persistent Dressmaker

Edinburgh's George Street was for some years the haunt of a graceful lady dressed beautifully in old-fashioned clothes. Passers-by would often stop and stare, for she seemed quite real. Her appearances caused a great deal of consternation for a while. Who was this lady, so elegant but out-of-date? The figure would glide along the street, quite oblivious of other pedestrians. She would always head for the same shop, disappearing in the doorway.

It transpired that the ghostly lady was one Mademoiselle Jane Vernelt. The shop had once been hers – a dressmaker's business that she had been forced to give up on account of precarious mental health. She must have been sorry to leave it, for after her death her ghost kept trying to return.

Holyrood Palace – Memories of Murder

There are two well-known supernatural phenomena associated with the Palace of Holyroodhouse, which graces the foot of the Royal Mile. Both bear relation to Mary Queen of Scots.

The first concerns the Italian, David Rizzio, with whom the young queen formed a close friendship when she arrived in Scotland. Mary's new husband, Lord Darnley, did not approve of the friendship and became increasingly jealous of his wife's closeness to Rizzio. With the support of some of the most powerful of Scotland's nobility, Darnley plotted against Rizzio. One night in 1566, Darnley and some of his co-conspirators burst into Mary's private apartments, grabbed Rizzio and stabbed him brutally and repeatedly. After his death, attempts were made to clean the floor of his bloodstains, but these were unsuccessful. The stains reappeared again and again, no matter how often the floor was scrubbed. They can still, some say, be seen to this day.

Darnley, of course, met an unpleasant end himself when his house at Kirk o' Field was blown up barely a year after the murder of Rizzio. He also left his mark on the Palace of Holyroodhouse, albeit in a less colourful manner than Rizzio. In one of the rooms that Darnley frequented at Holyrood, the apartment where he entertained his visitors, strange shadows have been seen many a time by visitors and staff. It seems as if someone is still there, hovering about the room.

Mary King's Close – Victims of the Plague

Edinburgh City Chambers, which stand on the Royal Mile, were built in the 1750s. Behind the City Chambers, the ground slopes steeply down towards The Mound and then to Princes Street. At either side of the City Chambers some closes of the Old Town still remain, their buildings clinging precariously to the steep slope. Beneath the City Chambers are the remains of another close, sixty-five yards or so of what was once a bustling, overcrowded street of traders in the early part of the seventeenth century. Hidden from the public eye for many years, the close is now a site for guided tours, which are proving to be popular with residents of the city and visitors alike.

Mary King's Close was particularly badly affected when plague hit Edinburgh in 1645. The plague was a horrifying disease. Scores of people died in the outbreak. Such was its severity that parliament moved from the capital city to Stirling. Attempts to isolate the sick and dying were largely fruitless, hygiene being poor or, some would say, non-existent. In the crammed dirty and rat-infested closes of Edinburgh the infection could spread rapidly. Desperate measures were called for to try to halt the rampaging disease, and one of these measures was to seal off Mary King's Close.

The plague passed, but the close remained sealed up. It would have remained uninhabited for ever, but some forty years later the need for accommodation in the already overpopulated city centre was becoming too pressing to ignore, so the city council gave its permission for the Close to be reopened. Some of the first residents were the family of Thomas Coltheart. Ignoring rumours of ghosts of the plague victims, the members of the family moved their belongings into one of the old houses, but they had hardly settled in before they found themselves regretting their decision. The atmosphere in their new home turned most unpleasant – spine-chillingly so. Then, all at once, a severed head appeared before the family, floating in mid-air. It was a grim, grey-haired, bearded old man – or at least, what was left of him.

This was the first of several apparitions. Over the coming days, the Colthearts were visited by a child's head, a severed arm and headless animals. At first, the family tried to pass these occurrences off as figments of imagination, but then stories began to circulate among other new residents to the close of strange happenings that bore a remarkable similarity to those in the Colthearts' home.

What happened after that is uncertain. Some say that the Colthearts fled in terror. Others say that they commanded the spirits to be at peace and then the family continued to live in the Close without further disturbance.

In later years, Mary King's Close was dreadfully damaged by fire. In 1753, work began on the City Chambers and the close ceased to exist. All the upper storeys and most of the buildings at ground level were demolished. All that remains is the small stretch beneath the offices above. But the ghost stories persist. Visitors and tour guides have heard strange noises, such as the noise of a small child crying. Some people have seen things. Quite a few visitors, unprompted, have spoken of seeing the figure of a little girl in one of the rooms. She is said to be small in stature, and dirty and dishevelled. Pustules, a sign of the plague, have been seen on her face. From time to time visitors who have seen the little girl or heard about her have left toys or sweets for her in a niche in the wall. As well as specific sightings such as this, there have been reports of visitors to Mary King's Close feeling 'cold spots' in certain places. The spectres of the past are still around.

Number 17 – The Room of Terror

Close to the Botanical Gardens, in a particularly attractive area of Edinburgh, is the site where once stood a row of houses, now demolished. One in particular, number 17, held a particularly gruesome secret.

Not long after the turn of the nineteenth century, when the house had lain empty for some years, it was bought by an enterprising husband and wife who wanted to use it as a boarding house. But it was not long before they noticed that one of the attic rooms had a strange and unpleasant atmosphere. People were reluctant to enter the room, let alone use it. Sometimes it seemed as if there was something, or someone, in the room. On one particular occasion a young girl who had been employed to help with the housekeeping went into the attic room only to re-emerge at once, screaming hysterically. She collapsed with the shock of whatever she had seen and when revived could not be enticed to put into words what had terrified her so.

Word soon spread about the room in number 17, and students at the university began to dare each other to take up residence there. The young man who finally took up the dare was named Andrew Muir. It is said that, rather than taking on the challenge out of bravado, this particular young man was quite religious and was interested from a spiritual point of view. He approached the owners of the house and offered to spend a night in the room. Anxious to put an end to the rumours of something dreadful going on in their boarding house, the owners agreed. They gave Andrew Muir a bell, along with strict instructions to sound the alarm if he saw or heard anything out of the ordinary. Then they bade him goodnight and good luck. The other inhabitants of the house made themselves ready for bed and retired for the night, leaving Andrew Muir to keep his lonely vigil in the attic room.

They were all in bed asleep, and everything was quiet when all of a sudden they were woken by the noise of the bell and an accompanying scream of fear and horror. They all jumped from their beds and rushed upstairs to the attic to find out what had happened. When they opened the door of the attic room, a terrible sight met their eyes – Andrew Muir lay dead with the bell at his side. On his face was a look of abject terror. He had seen something so awful, it would appear, that the life had literally been frightened out of him. After that, the attic room was never used again. The house was demolished some twenty years later.

Victoria Terrace – The Sad Spectre of Angus Roy

The story of Angus Roy is not one of dreadful deeds or sinister happenings. It is merely sad – the story of a man tormented and bullied to despair. Angus Roy was a sailor who lived at the beginning of the nineteenth century, serving on a ship that sailed out of the port of Leith. His sailing career was cruelly cut short by an accident from which he was lucky to have escaped with his life. He fell from the top of the ship's mast, and, although he miraculously survived, he was terribly badly injured. One leg was left virtually useless after the accident, dragging behind him as he limped along.

Angus came to live in Edinburgh's Victoria Terrace after his discharge from the merchant navy, but far from being able to live out what remained of his life in peace, he suffered continual torment at the hands of the local children. They teased and bullied him because of his disability, following him along the street, taunting him and calling him names. It was only after his death that Angus was able to exact some sort of revenge upon his tormentors. His ghost returned to haunt the area, a harmless spectre but frightening enough to have the effect of making those who had mistreated him regret their behaviour.

It is said that the sound of Angus Roy's damaged leg scraping along the ground behind him as he makes his way along the street is still heard from time to time around the area where he lived.

The West Bow – The Devilish Ghost of Major Weir

In the early part of the seventeenth century there lived in the West Bow of Edinburgh, along with his sister Grizel, one Major Thomas Weir. To all appearances, Major Weir was a worthy bachelor indeed – outwardly respectable, a veritable pillar of society. Deeply religious and knowledgeable about all things spiritual, he was a familiar figure at prayer meetings and gatherings, often playing a leading role. He was a large man of imposing appearance, and he was rarely seen without his 'trademark', a black staff. He seemed to be so reliant upon this black staff that people began to speculate that perhaps it possessed some sort of magical or spiritual power. The speculations were dismissed as foolish rumour, idle and fanciful gossip. It served no good to speak of a pious man like Thomas Weir in such a way.

In 1670, however, Major Weir, for no reason that anyone could fathom, did something that sent waves of shock through Edinburgh and eventually sealed his own death warrant. He made a confession, one that would give credence to any malicious rumours that might have circulated about him, and much more. Accustomed to addressing religious gatherings, he stood up at one particular meeting and prepared to speak. When he did speak, it was not the prayers that they had been expecting that his audience heard. It was a catalogue of the most heinous and sinful deeds imaginable, especially offensive to those of religious leanings. Major Weir accused himself of having lived in an incestuous relationship with his sister for years. He told of sharing with his sister in knowledge and practice of witchcraft, satanic rituals and necromancy. He claimed to have consorted with the devil himself.

The first reaction of his stunned audience was to assume that the Major had taken leave of his senses. These were the ravings of a madman, surely! Doctors were consulted, priests were sought out for their advice, but Weir persisted. His stories were consistent and detailed. He could not and would not be ignored. Doctors finally pronounced Major Weir to be sane. There was no option but to believe his stories.

Major Weir and his sister were both executed for crimes of witchcraft. Major Weir was strangled and then burnt, a standard means of execution for condemned witches at the time. His black staff was burnt with him. Onlookers at the time were to report that the staff took on a life of its own when subjected to the heat of the flames – it danced and squirmed in a most alarming fashion. Grizel was hanged. As an act of final defiance, she attempted to take all her clothes off on the scaffold, prompting the hangman to act more quickly than he might have preferred.

It was not long before people had signs that Major Weir had returned to his old haunts after his execution. His house remained unoccupied for the most part of the one hundred and fifty years following his death – it had unpleasant associations. For a while, it was inhabited by a family by the name of Patullo, but they soon left, alarmed by the strange apparitions that plagued them. Empty or not, however, the house often seemed full of life – sounds of raucous merrymaking and devilish laughter were heard coming from the building. Lights were seen in the house at night, giving it an eerie glow. The sound of Grizel's spinning wheel was reported to have been heard by several people.

The house was finally demolished in the first half of the nineteenth century, but Major Weir and his sister have never gone away. They continue to haunt the area around the West Bow, although the street as it once was, from Edinburgh Castle to Grassmarket, has long gone. The Major has been seen striding about the streets, swinging his staff as he walks. The sound of Grizel's spinning wheel can still be heard from time to time. Sometimes Major Weir is seen to ride out on a phantom black horse. And from time to time, it is said, the sound of galloping horses and clattering wheels can be heard as the devil himself comes riding in his coach for another assignation with Thomas and Grizel.

GHOSTLY CASTLES

Scotland is famous the world over for its castles, fortified homes of the great (but not necessarily good) of times gone by. Castles in various states of repair can be found in all parts of the country, from the Borders to the far north. Some are still inhabited; some are looked after by the National Trust for Scotland or Historic Scotland as visitor sites of historical interest; some lie in deserted ruins, inhabited only by the spirits of the dead who haunt them. There can hardly be one of these castles that does not have at least one ghostly story to tell.

Abergeldie Castle

The earliest parts of Abergeldie Castle, which stands barely two miles from the royal family's country home at Balmoral, date from the sixteenth century. The castle has had its fair share of visiting guests over the years, including royalty. It also has an extra, uninvited 'guest', known as French Kate or Kitty Rankie. She was apparently a French woman who was employed in the castle at one time. The unfortunate soul was suspected of practising black magic and was arrested and charged with witchcraft. She was confined in the castle until found guilty. Then she was taken to a neighbouring hill, tied to a stake and burnt for her crimes. Her angry spirit returned to the castle after her death.

Balgonie Castle

Balgonie Castle in Fife was originally built in the fourteenth century, with additions made to the structure over the following three centuries or so. In times gone by, the castle was the seat of the Earls of Leven, but gradually it fell into disrepair in the eighteenth and nineteenth centuries.

The present owners of the castle, the family of Raymond Morris, have worked hard at restoring Balgonie for over ten years. The ghost for which Balgonie is most famous has been seen by the laird and other members of his family, and also by visitors. She is known as Green Jeannie and has been seen mostly at night, particularly in a part of the castle that was constructed at the beginning of the eighteenth century. As her name suggests, the apparition is bright green in colour.

There have been other ghostly signs at Balgonie apart from Green Jeannie. Strange noises are heard from time to time, and shadowy figures have appeared, particularly in the area of the great hall of the castle.

Ballindalloch Castle

Ballindalloch Castle in Banffshire has quite a reputation for its ghosts. The castle dates from the sixteenth century and has been inhabited by the same family, the Grants and Macpherson-Grants, throughout its history. It is open to the public for some months of the year, and both the members of the family who live in the castle and members of the visiting public have testified to the presence of more than one ghost.

The Pink Tower, a bedroom in the castle, is the haunt of a beautiful lady dressed in a crinoline. Several visitors have seen her. She is a benign presence, and although those who see her might be startled initially, it soon becomes clear that the ghost means no harm.

The dining room, which was originally the great hall of the castle, has a ghost in the form of a green lady. Nobody knows who she is, but she has been seen on more than one occasion.

There is also a male ghost at Ballindalloch. He is thought to be General James Grant, a member of the family who died in 1806. He is buried close to the estate and is said to return there every night, riding a magnificent white horse. It is as if, even in death, he wishes to keep a proprietorial eye on his home and lands. His ghost also walks around the castle itself, making its way through a passage at the foot of the tower to the wine cellar, which was once upon a time the castle dungeon.

The fourth ghost associated with Ballindalloch has a sad story. Apparently, she was a family member who fell passionately in love, only to be rejected. Unable to accept that she had been spurned, she continued to write to the object of her desires, pleading for his attention. The pathetic vision of the young woman is seen from time to time crossing the old Bridge of Avon on her way to post another letter to her beloved. In more recent years, the old bridge was bypassed by a new one, and workmen engaged in the construction of the new bridge are reported to have seen the figure of the young woman several times.

Barcaldine Castle

Barcaldine Castle is one of two places haunted by a pair of Campbell brothers. Barcaldine, a stately sixteenth-century building, typically Scottish in appearance, stands in open countryside close to Loch Creran. The castle saw a brutal murder in the eighteenth century. The laird of Barcaldine was Donald Campbell, and for years he had been involved in a bitter feud with Stewart of Appin. The dispute came to an abrupt and bloody end when Stewart killed Donald Campbell with his sword.

Stewart knew that when his crime was found out, reprisals by the Campbells would be swift, bitter and painful. In order to ensure his own safety, he sought refuge at the home of Donald Campbell's brother, Duncan, at Inverawe. The news of the killing had not yet got out, so Donald Campbell offered Stewart his hospitality when he was asked for it, according to the custom in the Highlands of Scotland.

As long as Stewart of Appin stayed in his home, Duncan Campbell was haunted by visions of his brother, who admonished him for sheltering his murderer. By the time Campbell had heard the news of his brother's death and had realised that he had been seeing his dead brother's ghost, Stewart had gone.

Donald Campbell's ghost left Inverawe – his brother Duncan's ghost frequents that building – and returned to Barcaldine Castle. It still appears there from time to time, an angry spectre of a man cheated out of life and deprived of his brother's revenge by a wily Stewart.

Bedlay Castle

Bedlay Castle stands close to Glasgow, at Chryston. It was first built in the twelfth century as a palace for the bishops of Glasgow. The castle appears to have avoided notoriety until one day, around the year 1350, one Bishop Cameron had the misfortune to be found dead, floating face down in the waters of a nearby loch. The bishop, it would seem, had not gone willingly into the afterlife, for after his death he continued to appear in the castle in ghostly form.

The appearances of Bishop Cameron and the sounds that he made caused considerable torment to the inhabitants of the castle in the centuries to come, so much so that an exorcism was reported to have been attempted towards the end of the nineteenth century. It was unsuccessful.

In the nineteen seventies Castle Bedlay became home to an antique dealer and his family, and they claimed both to have seen the large figure of the bishop appearing before them and to have heard him pacing restlessly about in neighbouring rooms.

Braemar Castle

Braemar Castle is still used as a residence by the Farquharson family who have been in possession of the castle since shortly after it was built in the first half of the seventeenth century.

The female ghost that haunts Braemar is thought to be a particularly tragic figure who lost her life through a simple misunderstanding. It is said that over two hundred years ago a young couple came to the castle to spend their wedding night. In those days, of course, respectable young ladies were chaste and remained virgins until their wedding day. Many girls were left in a state of almost total ignorance when it came to sex. The wedding night, therefore, was likely to be approached with quite considerable apprehension, even fear, on the part of the bride. What would be expected of her? Would she make a 'good' wife?

The story goes that the young bride at Braemar woke quite early on the morning after her wedding night to find that she was alone in the bed. She got up and searched the apartments surrounding the bedroom but could find no sign of her new husband. She became very distressed when she could not find him and at once jumped to the conclusion that, having found her to be an unsatisfactory bed mate the night before, her husband had left her. Overcome with shame and confusion, the distraught young woman flung herself to her death from the window of the bridal room.

The poor girl had been sadly mistaken. Her new husband had not left her but had, instead, gone out hunting at crack of dawn while she was still sleeping.

When the bridegroom returned from his hunting trip and rode back into the castle courtyard, he was greeted with the terrible news that his beautiful young bride was dead. How he must have regretted departing without letting his sweetheart know where he was going!

The ghost of the young bride is said to return to the castle whenever newly-weds come to stay there. Whom does she wish to warn? Does she urge young brides not to jump to hasty conclusions, or does she want to remind the grooms that thoughtless behaviour will only lead to heartache?

Brodie Castle

Brodie Castle in Morayshire is now in the care of the National Trust for Scotland. It has been the seat of the Brodie family for many centuries, and in 1889 the family experienced something for which no rational explanation could be found.

The castle had been rented out for a while, as the Earl of Brodie was abroad, in Switzerland. One night in September, the butler at Brodie Castle told some of the other servants that he could hear noises coming from the Earl's study. It sounded as if someone was inside. When the other servants listened, they too could hear noises – moaning sounds and what sounded like pages being turned or papers being rustled. This was very odd, as the Earl had locked his study before his departure, leaving strict instructions that no one was to enter the room in his absence. Thinking that there might be an intruder, the servants searched for a key to the room but could find none.

The next day, news reached the castle that the Earl of Brodie had died in Switzerland the previous night. It could only be assumed that the Earl's ghost had returned to his study on the night of his death, perhaps with a wish to deal with outstanding business.

Buckholme Tower

Buckholme Tower, now in ruins, stands close to the Border town of Galashiels. Three centuries ago, it was the home of a terrible and tyrannical man, Laird Pringle. He had a violent temper and a sadistic nature. So abusive was he to his wife and son that they were forced to flee from Buckholme, leaving the laird to live alone, apart from the long-suffering servants on whom he vented his spleen with startling regularity.

As well as indulging in his fondness for large quantities of drink, Laird Pringle is said to have spent much of his time hunting. It would seem that blood sports were one way he used to express the cruel side of his nature. One night, however, he was offered the chance to hunt not animals, but humans.

The 1680s were years of much bloodshed in Scotland. It was the time of the Covenanters, strong Presbyterians who wanted to worship as they pleased, contrary to the laws passed by the parliament in England. Forced to meet in secret, they were constantly being hounded by the Redcoat forces, driven out of their hiding places and punished most cruelly.

Pringle hated the Covenanters, and when he was called upon to assist a band of Redcoats intent on raiding a secret Covenanters' meeting on the moor near his home, he was delighted to help. He called his ferocious hunting hounds to heel and set off on horseback.

The Redcoats were too late. Someone must have warned the Covenanters, for their meeting had broken up and they had fled. The 'hunting' expedition was not entirely fruitless, however, for in the course of their search, the troops came upon one old man and his son, hiding nearby. The old man had fallen and injured his back and had been unable to escape, so his son had stayed by his side. The pair could not deny that they were Covenanters, for to do so was to deny God.

Pringle would have killed the two of them then and there, but the officer in charge of the Redcoat troops prevented him from doing so. The captives were to face a proper trial, he insisted. Besides, they were of more use alive than dead, since with a little 'persuasion' they might be induced to share some useful information with their captors. Pringle was to take them back to Buckholme Tower and hold them there to await further questioning and subsequent trial.

Pringle dragged the two men back to Buckholme and threw them into the cellar. The laird's sadism and thirst for blood were, however, stronger than any respect he might have had for the law. Later that night, his servants heard him lurching drunkenly down to the cellar. They listened with great apprehension.

Sounds of a scuffle could be heard, then crashes and thumps, roars and screams of agony. Too terrified of their master to take any action, the servants could only listen outside the door and wait. The screaming stopped. The laird stumbled out of the cellar, covered in blood and triumphant.

'Swine should be treated as swine!' he raged, shoving his men aside as he made his way unsteadily upstairs again. When he reached the entrance hall, he was met by a local woman standing at the door. She was the old man's wife and had come to beg for the release of her husband and son. Laird Pringle dragged her down to the cellar and threw open the door to reveal what was inside. There, suspended on the wall, iron hooks through their jaws just like two slaughtered pigs, were the man and the boy.

Pringle watched with obvious relish as the woman subsided into hysterical sobbing. Then, after a few moments, she composed herself and turned to face the laird. She cursed him for what he had done. Just as his hounds had hunted down the Covenanters, his awful deeds would come back like the hounds of hell and hunt him down for eternity.

For the first time in a long time, Pringle was really frightened. For the remainder of his life he was tormented by visions of ghostly hounds, their teeth bared, saliva dripping from their jaws as they moved in for the attack. After his death, people began to hear the strangest sounds at night – the baying of hounds on the hunt and the agonised screams of a man in fear for his life.

Although the rest of Buckholme Tower lies in ruins, the cellar remains. Sometimes at night, it is said, you can still hear the noise of dogs and of Laird Pringle's tormented screams.

The Castle of Mey

The Castle of Mey, Highland home of Her Royal Majesty Queen Elizabeth the Queen Mother, stands in the very far north of Scotland, a few miles from John o' Groats. The castle is haunted by a green lady who appears in a room at the top of the old tower. She is said to be the ghost of a young woman of the Sinclair family. She fell in love with a local lad, a farmworker. A lad such as this, of the humblest of origins, was considered by the girl's father to be a most undesirable suitor for his daughter. He sought to put an end to the relationship and confined his daughter to the tower until she saw sense. It is said that when the girl leaned out of the window to try to catch a glimpse of her sweetheart working in the fields in the distance, she lost her balance, toppled over and fell to her death from the tower.

Cawdor Castle

Cawdor Castle is the haunt of a female ghost – a woman with no hands. The castle stands a few miles from Nairn. It was built in 1370 and became a seat of the Campbell family around 1510–11. The ghost does not date from the early times but from the first half of the nineteenth century, not long after the head of the family became entitled to call himself Earl of Cawdor. It is thought that the ghost was once the daughter of an Earl of Cawdor who found herself smitten with a young man from a rival family. The Earl of Cawdor discovered the secret romance when he came upon the sweethearts one day in their secret meeting place. The Earl was infuriated by his daughter's treachery. He cut her hands off with his sword so that she might never embrace her lover again.

Claypotts Castle

Claypotts Castle in its present form was built at the end of the sixteenth century by John Strachan and his son Gilbert. In 1625, Claypotts passed into the hands of Sir William Graham of Claverhouse. The castle stayed in the Graham family for three generations, and in 1672 it came into the possession of John Graham of Claverhouse, Viscount Dundee, known as Bonnie Dundee. John Graham had achieved considerable notoriety for his actions against the Covenanters. Another nickname, coined no doubt by some of those who held him in particular contempt for what he had done, was Bluidy Clavers.

Many stories were circulated about Claverhouse, and who knows if they had any foundation in reality. It is known that although Claypotts was not his main residence, Graham did stay there from time to time. In the area surrounding Claypotts, rumours spread about his activities whilst in residence. He was said to have consorted with witches and warlocks, and wild orgies were reputed to have taken place at the castle. Some people believed that it was at Claypotts that John Graham of Claverhouse bargained with the devil for mystical powers. These powers were said to have made him, amongst other things, bullet-proof. Legend has it that at the Battle of Killiecrankie, where Graham finally met his end, he was killed not by a bullet but by a silver button from the uniform of an enemy soldier.

Years after the death of Bonnie Dundee, it is said that at Halloween Claypotts Castle was seen to glow with the lights of demonic fires and that sounds of revelry of the blackest kind could be heard.

On 29 May every year, it is said that a white lady appears at an upstairs window in Claypotts Castle. The White Lady appears to be very distressed and is waving a white handkerchief. This ghost is supposed to be Marion Ogilvy, who was the daughter of the first Lord Airlie. The story goes that she was in love with Cardinal Beaton of St Andrews. She would wait at the window for him to arrive and wave her handkerchief as a signal to him. On 29 May 1546, the lady waited in vain, for Cardinal Beaton lay in St Andrews Castle, murdered. On the anniversary of his death, every year, the White Lady resumes her vigil.

This story presents certain difficulties. The castle in its present form, and the window from which the White Lady is said to wave, would not yet have been built in 1546. Furthermore, Marion Ogilvy did not actually live at Claypotts. Her home was in Melgund Castle. Thirdly, Cardinal Beaton is not known to have had anything to do with Claypotts at all. If he ever visited the place, there seems to be no record of him having done so. So how did the story start and who is the White Lady?

Comlongon Castle

Comlongon Castle in Dumfriesshire has a green lady ghost that dates from the late sixteenth century. She is the tragic figure of Marion Carruthers, who was being coerced into marrying a man she did not love. Having taken refuge at her uncle's home at Comlongon, she finally despaired of the situation and threw herself from the tower of the castle.

Cortachy Castle

Cortachy Castle, north of Kirriemuir in Angus, is the family seat of the Ogilvy clan. To this day the castle is said to be haunted by the ghost of a drummer but only on certain ominous occasions. Whenever the drumbeat is heard, so they say, a death in the Ogilvy family is imminent.

The phantom drummer is said to be the ghost of a drummer at Cortachy who incurred the wrath of his master. There is more than one version of how this came to be so, but one story tells that the drummer failed to give warning when the castle was about to be attacked. As fitting punishment, the negligent drummer was dragged to the top of the tower and flung to his death, along with his drum. The Cortachy drummer has been heard not only at Cortachy but also elsewhere as, so it is said, when members of the family have been abroad. The sound of the phantom drumming strikes fear into the hearts of the Ogilvy family, for it can mean only one thing – tragedy is about to strike.

Craigievar Castle

Craigievar Castle is now a National Trust for Scotland property. It stands near Alford in Aberdeenshire and dates from the early seventeenth century. The castle is home to a number of ghosts, so it is said.

The Blue Room in the tower is reputedly haunted by a member of the Gordon clan who fell from the window there. He was forced to his death at sword-point by 'Red' Sir John Forbes, a man of some notoriety. People have heard the footsteps of the unfortunate Gordon climbing the steps to the Blue Room, as if re-enacting the moments before his death.

One of the other ghosts at Craigievar is said to be very selective in his appearances. It is thought that he is the ghost of a musician, a fiddler who fell into the well at the castle and drowned. He is said to appear only to those who bear the name of Forbes.

Crathes Castle

Crathes Castle, the home of the Burnett family until it became a National Trust for Scotland property, can be found a few miles from the small town of Banchory in the northeast of Scotland. Earliest building work on the castle dates from the middle of the sixteenth century, with additions having been made in the early part of the seventeenth century and in the eighteenth century.

In the oldest part of the castle, the double tower, there is a room known as the Green Lady's Room because of the frequent sightings of such a phenomenon over many years. The identity of the Green Lady is uncertain, although some people believe her to have been one of the family. She has been seen both on her own and with a baby. The existence of such a woman in real time has been borne out by the fact that during restoration work in the building two skeletons were discovered, one of a woman, the other of a baby. It is thought to be most likely that the woman had become pregnant in undesirable circumstances and that someone had taken the decision that it would be most prudent to avoid embarrassment to the family and dispose of both mother and baby. In spite of her remains having been freed from their place of hiding, the Green Lady continues to haunt the tower.

Delgatie Castle

Delgatie Castle is a tower house of considerable historical interest, dating from the sixteenth century. The tower has one ghost, said to be a female with red hair, who has startled people there on several occasions, including a number of troops billeted at the castle during the Second World War.

Drumlanrig Castle

Drumlanrig Castle is a handsome edifice in Dumfriesshire, which was built in the seventeenth century for the first Duke of

Queensberry, William Douglas. He himself spent very little time at the castle, but his family used the castle as a residence for more than a hundred years, after which time it became the property of the Dukes of Buccleuch.

One ghost that haunts Drumlanrig Castle is that of a headless woman – not strictly headless, perhaps, for she does have a head, only it is not attached to her shoulders. She carries it about with her in her hands. It is thought that perhaps she is the ghost of Lady Anne Douglas, but how the ghost came to be decapitated is a mystery.

The other well-known ghost at Drumlanrig is a particularly unusual one – a yellow monkey. This creature, unattractive in appearance and disturbingly large by all accounts, can be seen in one particular room of the castle, which is given the name, in very early castle records, of the Yellow Monkey or Haunted Room. Nobody has any knowledge of where such a beast might have come from or if there ever was such an unusual pet at the castle, but over the years there have been several sightings of the hairy creature.

Dunstaffnage Castle

Dunstaffnage Castle, near Oban in Argyll, dates from the thirteenth century and is now preserved by Historic Scotland. Various ghostly figures have put in appearances here, including one of several green lady ghosts that are said to inhabit various places in Scotland. The Green Lady is thought to be a glaistig, and her appearances, always associated with poltergeist activity around the castle, are thought to be omens of notable occurrences, either good or bad.

Duntrune Castle

Duntrune Castle in Argyll stands in a spectacular setting overlooking Loch Crinan. In the seventeenth century it was a seat of the Campbell clan. Close to the beginning of the century, an Irishman, Coll Ciotach, brought his troops over to Scotland with the intent of waging war upon the Campbells, whom he hated. Unwilling to risk attacking Duntrune without prior knowledge of its defences or of the number of enemy soldiers he would have to face, he sent his piper ahead to try to gain the confidence of the Campbells and discover the information that was required. Pipers were privileged in Highland society and could be guaranteed hospitality wherever they went in return for a few good tunes. Coll's plan was therefore both devious and cunning.

The piper duly approached the castle and was admitted by the Campbells, but their suspicions were soon aroused. The piper seemed unduly curious about the place and asked too many questions. It would be wrong to kill him, for they had no proof that he was up to no good. Besides, they had offered him their hospitality. By way of compromise, they locked him in one of the tower rooms to prevent him from escaping while they decided what to do.

Not far from the castle, Coll's troops remained in hiding, waiting for the piper to return with the information that would help them to victory. But time passed and still the piper did not return. His men grew restive, and at length Coll lost patience. He decided to advance on the castle regardless. The piper, meanwhile, up in his tower room, was only too well aware of the dangers his master would be facing. The Campbell troops outnumbered Coll's forces and Duntrune was strong and well defended. He had to give warning to Coll somehow.

Very bravely, he took up his pipes and began to play an alarm. Coll's troops retreated at once, but the piper had signed his own death warrant. The Campbells had heard the sound of his pipes and realised what he was up to. They stormed up to the tower room and dragged the poor musician out. His fingers were cut from his hands and he was left to bleed to death.

The piper's remains were interred elsewhere in the castle. Years later, it is said, the fingerless skeleton was discovered and given a religious burial. In spite of the fact that the piper's body has been put properly to rest, his spirit will not let Duntrune forget the cruelty of the Campbells. The piper's ghostly playing can still be heard in the tower room, and strange occurrences, similar to the activities of a poltergeist, have been reported. They too are thought to be attributable to the spirit of Coll's brave piper.

Duntulm Castle

Duntulm Castle in the north of the island of Skye now stands in ruins, but its colourful history assures it of the presence of more than one ghost.

One of the ghosts is said to have been the reason why the castle ceased to be used for habitation in the early eighteenth century. The ghost is that of Hugh, Uisdean Gillespie Chleirich, who was the cousin of Donald Gorm Mor, chief of the MacDonalds of Sleat. Donald Gorm Mor was an unpopular and brutal chief and had his fair share of enemies. Hugh was perhaps the most deadly of these enemies and had long plotted to kill Donald Gorm Mor, one such plot being made known to Donald Gorm Mor. There are different versions of the story, so it is not clear exactly how this happened, but Donald, having been informed of his cousin's treachery, set about getting his revenge. He laid siege to Hugh's castle, hoping to starve him out. Hugh escaped, disguised as a woman, but he was soon captured by Donald Gorm Mor's men and taken to Duntulm. There he was locked (one version of the story tells that he was bricked up) in a dungeon. But the confinement of his enemy was not enough to satisfy Donald Gorm Mor's appetite for revenge. He saw to it that Hugh suffered cruelly for his treachery. Hugh's only means of survival in the dungeon were meagre rations of salt meat and salt fish. No water was given to him. Needless to say, he died a slow and painful death from dehydration. His screams were said to haunt the castle continuously after his death, causing great torment to all within.

Another ghost that haunted Duntulm was that of Margaret, a ward of the previous chief, Donald Gorm. After Donald Gorm's death, she was placed, according to his dying wishes, in the care of Donald Gorm Mor until she came of age. When she came of age, she was to marry Donald Gorm Mor or enter a convent. According to one source, Margaret was hopelessly in love with Hugh and devastated by his cruel fate at the hands of Donald Gorm Mor. According to another source, Margaret was cruelly rejected by Donald Gorm Mor, principally because she had only one eye. For whatever reasons, Margaret's life was an unhappy one. She did not marry Donald Gorm Mor and eventually entered a convent, but she died soon afterwards. Her ghost returned to Duntulm and could be heard weeping around the castle for many years after her death.

Donald Gorm Mor himself was also said to haunt Duntulm in the company of two drunken friends. The three ghostly figures proved to be quite a trial for Donald Gorm Mor's successor, his nephew, Donald Gorm Mor Og.

Two more ghosts haunted the castle – those of a tiny heir and his nursemaid. It is said that the baby fell from the nurse's arms out of a window high in the castle and onto rocks below, where he died. The baby's father, enraged with pain and grief, ordered that the nurse be tied up and set adrift in a leaking boat. The cries of the baby and his nurse can still be heard in the ruins of the castle and on the rocks where the poor infant met his death.

Dunvegan Castle

Dunvegan Castle on the Isle of Skye is famous not for haunting as such but for the precious Fairy Flag, which is kept in the castle. An extremely old, discoloured and worn piece of material, it hardly resembles a flag at all, but it is said to possess remarkable supernatural power. Dunvegan is the seat of the MacLeod clan, and their attachment to the Fairy Flag stems from the ancient belief that, if the MacLeod family is ever in dire peril, the flag, if unfurled, will protect them from harm. This superstition has been given weight by the fact that on two separate occasions in history, the flag was unfurled in battle and the MacLeod clan and their soldiers were able to overcome their enemies in spite of what had seemed to be insurmountable odds.

How the flag came into the possession of the family is a matter of some debate, but one story tells of a party in the castle many years ago. The nursemaid who was left in charge of the baby of the family left the child for a few moments to watch the revelries, and while she was gone the child kicked off its covers. When the nurse returned, she found that the child had been covered up by the fairies with the Fairy Flag. When she picked up the child in its new silken cover, fairy voices were heard telling the MacLeod family that if ever the flag was unfurled in battle the enemy would see twice as many MacLeod clansmen as were actually facing them. The flag could only be used three times, for whoever tried to use it a fourth time would disappear, along with the flag.

The Fairy Flag has been used twice, and no one would want to have to use it a third and final time, but its very presence in Dunvegan is considered by many to be some sort of lucky talisman in itself.

Ethie Castle

Ethie Castle, about five miles from the town of Arbroath, is now the home of the Forsyth family. The castle as it stands today dates from the early fifteenth century, but there was undoubtedly another building on the site before the present one was constructed.

Cardinal Beaton, abbot of Arbroath in the fifteenth century, commissioned the building of the present castle, and his ghost is said to haunt the place still. He lived at Ethie for several years, and Marion Ogilvy, his mistress, also lived there.

Cardinal Beaton was a powerful figure in the Catholic church and a fierce persecutor of those of the Protestant faith. He had many enemies. His life came to a violent end in St Andrews on 29 May 1546, when he was brutally murdered by Protestant nobles in the castle there.

The ghost of Cardinal Beaton parades slowly round Ethie Castle, particularly in the area close to his bedchamber. The sound of Cardinal Beaton's footsteps is quite unmistakable – his gouty leg thumps and scrapes as it drags along the passageways behind him.

There was another ghost at Ethie Castle – that of a young child. The child could be heard crying sometimes at night. In addition to this, witnesses had heard what sounded like a wheeled toy being pulled across the floor in one particular room in the castle. Eventually, investigations were carried out to discover the source of the strange sounds. A small skeleton was discovered and, alongside it, the remains of a toy wooden cart. The skeleton was removed from the castle and given a Christian burial. The ghost of the child was no longer heard at Ethie.

Fyvie Castle

Fyvie Castle in Aberdeenshire was once the haunt of a green lady who is now, it is thought, finally at peace in the afterlife. Her appearances began sometime around 1920 after a strange and unpleasant fungal mass appeared on one of the walls in the castle's gun room. The owner of the castle, Lord Leith, brought in builders to put matters to rights, and when they removed part of the wall, they discovered a skeleton. The skeleton was removed from the area and the haunting of the Green Lady began. Anxious to put a stop to the disturbing appearances of the Green Lady, the laird insisted that the skeleton be replaced behind the wall, which was then rebuilt. This might have seemed a little bizarre, but it turned out to have the desired effect. Behind the wall was just where this mysterious phantom wanted to be, it would appear, for she stopped causing any trouble to the inhabitants of the castle from that time onwards.

Gight Castle

Gight Castle in Aberdeenshire has a story attached to it that is almost identical to the story of the ghostly piper of Edinburgh Castle. The piper is said to have entered a secret tunnel, playing his pipes, and never to have returned. Gight Castle dates from the fifteenth century, but there seems to be no record of the year, or century, in which the piper was supposed to have disappeared. As is the case with the piper in Edinburgh Castle, there is no mention of anyone having gone into the tunnel to look for the poor fellow after he disappeared! A third version of this tale is told in connection with Culross Abbey.

Glamis Castle

Glamis Castle, a monstrous edifice with looming towers and a gloomy atmosphere, looks as if it ought to be haunted, and haunted it is, perhaps more so than any other place in Scotland. It is now the family seat of the Bowes-Lyons, Earls of Strathmore. Queen Elizabeth the Queen Mother, then Elizabeth Bowes-Lyon, lived at Glamis as a child, and in 1930, Princess Margaret, sister of Queen Elizabeth II, was born there. The castle, although peaceful now, has a colourful past and from time to time spectres from that past return to haunt the living.

Both a grey lady and a white lady have been seen to wander the castle. The Grey Lady is most frequently seen around the area of the chapel and there seems to be no definite idea as to her identity. The White Lady, who appears very infrequently, is thought to be the ghost of Janet Douglas, who lived in the sixteenth century and was the wife of John, sixth Lord Glamis. John died and Janet remarried, settling with her new husband, Campbell of Skipness, at Glamis. The king at the time, James V, hated the Douglas clan, the powerful family to which Janet belonged. As an act of what only can be construed as pure obsessive hatred, James had Janet captured and imprisoned in Edinburgh Castle on charges of witchcraft and conspiracy to poison the king. Her husband and son were imprisoned along with her. After several years' imprisonment, Janet was burned at the stake on Castle Hill. Her husband died in a bungled attempt to flee from the castle, and her son, Lord Glamis, was kept imprisoned until after the death of James V.

Ghastly stories are also told of what befell the Ogilvie family at

Glamis Castle in its early days. The Ogilvies were engaged in a bitter and deadly dispute with the Lindsay family, and one day found themselves having to call upon Lord Glamis for refuge. He duly let them into the castle and hid them, as they thought, safely in a secret chamber within the walls. Unfortunately, the Ogilvies had not chosen as safe a sanctuary as they had hoped. Lord Glamis had no intention of letting them out again, for, like the Lindsays, he too despised them. His treatment of them was, whatever he might have felt for them, grossly barbaric. He locked the door of the secret chamber and turned away, never to return. The poor members of the Ogilvie family were left to starve to death and rot in their hidden location

Nothing more was known of the fate of the Ogilvies until centuries later when one Earl of Strathmore accidentally happened upon the room in which the Ogilvies had been condemned to live out their last, painful days. It is said that when the Earl opened the door and discovered the rotted, skeletal contents of the hidden chamber, he fainted with horror and disgust.

'Beardie' is another ghost of Glamis, with a story that is also linked to the existence of some sort of hidden chamber. Accounts differ as to exactly who Beardie was. Some say he was the first Lord of Glamis, others that he was in fact the Earl of Crawford. Whichever he was (and still is, by all accounts), the story goes that he was a gambling man with a violent temper. Unable to find anyone to play cards with him late one Saturday night as the sacred Sabbath approached, Beardie announced that he would quite happily play with the devil himself if challenged so to do.

Right on cue, a dark stranger appeared and offered to take Beardie on in a card game. The two men retired to a chamber to play. The servants in the castle were intrigued by the noises of shouting and swearing they could hear coming from the room – it appeared that Beardie was losing and losing badly at that. One servant, unable to contain his curiosity, put his eye to the keyhole only to jump back screaming in pain, having been blinded by a shooting dart of flame.

Beardie emerged from the chamber, raging at the interruption. When he stormed back into the room to continue the game, the stranger had disappeared.

The devil had gone, but he had taken with him the soul of Beardie, which the rash lord had gambled away. It seemed as if Beardie was condemned to play cards for eternity, for after his death, some five years later, the room was in constant turmoil with the sounds of cursing, swearing card-players. The story goes that after some years, the chamber was sealed up in an attempt to stop the activities of the phantom Beardie, but his ghost, a fearsome creature complete with straggly beard, is still said to appear in certain places in the castle from time to time and the sounds of raucous card-playing can still, on occasion, be heard.

The first black ghost in Scotland is said to live in Glamis Castle. He is said to be the spirit of a much abused servant boy and is sometimes seen sitting on a stone seat just outside the Queen Mother's sitting room. Some say the child was ordered to sit there and wait until he was told what to do next. Terrified at the thought of the consequences of disobedience, the little boy did just that, but was forgotten about and left there overnight. Being a very lowly servant, he was poorly clad, especially for the rigours of the Scottish climate, and having been left to sit in a freezing corridor for hours on end, he died from hypothermia.

Other ghosts that have been seen at Glamis Castle include the gruesome apparition of a woman with no tongue, who flits across the grounds with her mouth open and bloody; a dark figure dressed in what appears to be a military coat; and a fleeting figure who is seen in the grounds (albeit briefly, for he runs so fast), known as Jack the Runner. The woman with no tongue is thought to have been witness to some ghastly deed and to have had her tongue cut out to ensure that she kept her silence. Just who the other two might be, nobody knows.

The greatest intrigue at Glamis concerns another secret room story and a monster story. At some time there is supposed to have existed, locked up in a secret chamber somewhere within the walls of Glamis Castle, a monster. Accounts vary as to just who or what the monster is supposed to have been and when it came into being, but all seem to indicate that the monster was in fact a family member. There are theories that the monster was in some way connected to Patrick, third Earl of Strathmore. Those who follow this line of thinking point to a picture of Patrick that hangs in the castle. In the painting, at Earl Patrick's side is an armour-clad figure of unknown identity, which looks as if its arms and body are strangely deformed. The theory does not make a lot of sense, for if the monster was so terrible that it had to be kept hidden away from the outside world under lock and key, why did the Earl of Strathmore have it included in a painting?

Other accounts of the existence of a monster, or at least a grossly deformed human being, suggest that the creature might have been the first son of the eleventh Earl of Strathmore. The twelfth Earl, Thomas, was born in 1822, but records apparently show that another son was born to the eleventh Earl and his wife in 1821, a son who supposedly died just after birth. The story goes that this son did not in fact die but was so horribly deformed that the family had to keep him hidden from public view. The child's younger brothers did not even know of his existence until they came of age, when, as a sort of gruesome rite of passage, they were each allowed to discover the location of the secret room. When they had been taken there, the awful truth was revealed to them. The secret of that hidden chamber was never revealed to any woman apparently, and was known only by three men at any one time. Those who became privy to the secret were said to have been shocked to the core – changed men from that day onwards.

Rumour has it that the monster lived until about 1921 – if he was born in 1821, he reached the age of a hundred, a surprisingly ripe old age for someone to live to at the turn of the nineteenth century. If the monster was born around the time of Patrick, the third Earl, then the theory defies belief.

Tales of the existence of a secret room hidden within the walls of the castle, for whatever purpose, are quite believable, for in places the walls are as much as four metres thick. Visitors to the castle have been known to try to find the location of the room by hanging towels out of the windows of all the rooms that they could find. In theory, the one window without a towel hanging from it would be the window of the secret room.

Some say that the location of the secret room is still known and that still only three people living at any one time are privy to the secret. Whatever the contents of the secret room – monster, monstrous remains or something else – its story has attracted a great deal of interest and much speculation over the years. Visitors to the castle at various times in the past century and before have made claims that their sleep has been disturbed by the most awful sights and sounds. And to this day there is a walkway on the roof, known as the Mad Earl's Walk, which is rumoured to be haunted by terrible noises. Here, it is said, the poor creature, the dreadful, hideous family secret, was taken under cover of darkness for exercise.

Hermitage Castle

Hermitage Castle, built in the mid-thirteenth century, stands in moorland south of the Border town of Hawick. Its rather bleak situation makes it a fitting site for ghostly haunts. Little remains of the building except a shell, but it does not take much imagination to conjure up pictures of all the things that might be lurking in its gloomy shadows.

Its grim history is recalled by the appearances of two spectral figures in particular. The first ghost is that of Sir Alexander Ramsay, Sheriff of Teviotdale, who, in 1342 incurred the wrath of Sir William Douglas, Knight of Liddesdale. The two had once been brothers in arms, but when King David II conferred the sheriffdom upon Ramsay, Douglas, who felt he had some claim to the title, was incensed. The unfortunate Ramsay was captured by Douglas in Hawick, taken to Hermitage and thrown into a dungeon in the castle. There he was left to starve to death. He was said to have tried to prolong his life by eating the few grains of corn that fell into the dungeon from the granary above. The sad, hungry figure of Sir Alexander Ramsay wanders around the ruins of the castle still.

The second ghost that is said to haunt Hermitage Castle is that of Lord Soulis – 'Bad Lord Soulis' or 'Terrible William'. Lord Soulis had a ghastly reputation indeed, for it was widely believed that he practised black magic and used the dungeons of the castle to hold young children from the surrounding area captive before incorporating them into his hideous rituals and eventually murdering them. He finally faced justice at the hands of his neighbours. People from the surrounding area gathered in force and stormed the castle, taking him captive and binding him in chains. We are told that he was wrapped in lead and then thrown into a boiling cauldron to meet a horribly painful death.

Another version of the story of Terrible William says that he had entered into a pact with the devil. He traded his soul in return for a licence to live however he pleased, indulging in whatever debaucheries took his fancy. Then, as he grew older and faced up to the inevitability of his approaching death, he panicked at the thought of the fiery furnaces of hell. It was in order to protect him from this fate that he was wrapped in lead and boiled by loyal subjects. This story, however, seems even less credible than the first one.

The figure of Terrible William has been seen around the grounds of the castle, and the screams of the children whom he abused so cruelly are also heard from time to time.

Linlithgow Palace

The stately ruins of Linlithgow Palace are now a popular visitor site, protected by Historic Scotland. In days gone by, Linlithgow was a much favoured royal palace. King James V of Scotland, who was born at Linlithgow in 1512, was said to have been particularly attached to the palace and he stayed there for long periods during his reign.

Linlithgow Palace is said to be haunted by the ghost of James V's wife, Mary of Guise. The ghost is seen in Queen Margaret's bower.

Littledean Tower

Littledean Tower stands close to the village of Maxton in Roxburghshire. The building dates from the fifteenth century. It has long been uninhabited, but it was at one time the stronghold of the Kerr family. One laird of Littledean, who lived in the tower in the seventeenth century, had a particularly bad reputation.

The laird was by all accounts a thoroughly unsavoury character. He drank heavily, mistreated his family and servants, and took great pleasure in playing an active part in the persecution of Covenanters in the district. He had a violent temper, and it is said that on one occasion he became so angry with a stable lad who had saddled and harnessed his horse improperly that he trampled the poor lad to death.

The laird enjoyed entertaining his friends – the only people who could bear his company were those who shared his liking for excess and bad behaviour – and they spent many raucous evenings drinking themselves incapable.

The laird's wife, Margaret, lived a miserable life. Her husband was undeniably cruel in his treatment of her. It seems, however, that she bore it all for the most part with remarkable dignity and stoicism. One evening, however, the laird overstepped the mark. He had, as usual, been drinking heavily with his companions, and one of them asked where Margaret was (it was her habit to keep well out of the way of her husband and his cronies at such times).

The laird dragged Margaret from her room and down to the dining hall where his visitors sat. He then proceeded to berate her and humiliate her in front of them. Margaret stood, confined by her husband's vicious grip on her arm, and suffered this treatment in silence.

At length the laird let her go, uttering as a final insult that he would rather be married to a woman from hell, for such a wife would have more warmth than the woman he had married.

It was a terrible thing to say, and Margaret finally broke her silence in response to it.

'You will live to regret these words,' she said, before quietly leaving the room.

The laird's friends bade him goodnight and left Littledean, but the laird was too fired up with drink and bad temper to settle. He saddled up his horse and rode off into the darkness. After some time, he came to a cottage in a clearing in the woods. The door was open and the laird could see a woman inside, sitting at a spinning wheel. He dismounted and approached. His horse seemed strangely agitated as the laird got to the cottage door, and he had to hold its reins very firmly to prevent it from bolting. Looking into the cottage, the laird thought that he could see shadowy figures moving in the corners, but it was too dark to make out what they were. He tried to speak to the woman. She did not respond in words to his greeting. Instead, she stopped spinning and turned to face him, still holding the newly spun thread between her fingers. With a maniacal laugh, she snapped the thread in two.

The laird saw no more, for at that point his horse took such fright and pulled him away with such force that he almost had to let go of the reins. He regained control of the animal at last, mounted and rode away. When he eventually arrived back at Littledean, he still had the picture of the woman in his mind. She had been the most beautiful creature he had ever laid eyes on.

The next day he found that in spite of himself he was preoccupied with the woman in the cottage. He set off to try to find her. He rode for most of the day, trying to find the same path through the wood that he had taken the night before, but in spite of many hours' searching he was unable to find any sign of the cottage where he had last seen the woman. He returned to Littledean, frustrated. As he approached his home, however, he caught sight of a graceful figure standing in a glade by the river – it was the very woman for whom he had been searching! She held out her arms to him in silence, and he went to her eagerly.

The laird's obsession with the woman grew. Every night at the same time, just before dark, she would appear at the same place by the river. His desire for her was so great that the laird ignored any need for caution. There, within sight of his marital home, he indulged his passion for this strange woman night after night.

It was inevitable that the affair would not remain a secret. The laird was seen with the woman and Lady Margaret was told about it. She confronted him and threw her wedding ring in his face. The laird merely turned on his heel and walked away.

Lady Margaret was ready to leave, but before she did she wanted to find out who her husband's mysterious lover was. Two men volunteered to go and search for the woman on her behalf. That evening they went to the glade by the river where the laird and the woman had been meeting, and after some time they caught sight of her. As they moved towards her stealthily, hoping to entrap her, she disappeared. A hare sped away from the place where she had been seen and ran far off into the distance.

The two men returned to Lady Margaret to find her in a state of great consternation. The laird was missing. There was little point in mounting a search at this late hour, for it was too dark. They had no choice but to wait.

It was far into the night when the laird's horse finally galloped up to the tower, carrying its master. The horse was sweating and exhausted; the laird was grim-faced and as white as a sheet. He was shaking as he told all those present what had happened to him. He had been riding towards home when he had caught sight of a hare running alongside his horse. Before long, the hare had been joined by several others, racing along beside him, in front of him and behind him. They leaped around the feet of his horse and jumped up to saddle height. The laird had been very frightened and had tried first to spur his horse on to outrun them, then to cut them down with his sword and trample them with the horse's hooves. His efforts were in vain until his sword struck the paw of one hare, cutting it clean off. The paw had jumped in the air and landed in the his pistol holster. The pack of hares had then suddenly withdrawn.

By the time all this had happened, the laird had ridden all the way to the village of Midlem, a place notorious for witchcraft and many miles from his home. He had spurred his horse into a gallop and had neither stopped nor even slowed his pace until he reached the safety of Littledean.

'Devils,' he muttered through chattering teeth. 'Devils!'

When he had told his tale, the laird put his hand into the pistol holster to feel for the hare's paw. He screamed, quickly withdrawing his hand from the holster and throwing something down on the ground.

'It grabbed me!' he cried.

Lady Margaret looked down at the thing that her husband had thrown from his holster. It was not a hare's paw but the bloody severed hand of a woman!

The laird drew his sword and speared the hand. As he did so, it flexed, very much as if it were alive. The laird took it, still impaled on his sword, out of the tower and made for the river. When he reached the water's edge, he hurled the bloody hand into the river's murky depths with all his might. He was very close to the spot where he and the mysterious woman had been meeting, and when he had thrown the hand in the river, he turned around and saw her, crouching beneath a tree. She lifted her head to look at him. To his horror, the laird saw that her face had been transformed into a hideous, wizened countenance with an evil leer.

'You took my hand from me,' she rasped. 'Now it will be with you for ever!'

The laird returned to the tower, still shaking. He collapsed into a chair by the fireside and put his hand into his pocket. The hand was there again! He threw it from the window in disgust and stumbled up to his bedchamber, hoping to find relief in sleep. But when he got into bed, he realised that he could feel something beneath the pillow on which his head lay. Putting his hand under the pillow, he withdrew the hideous hand. By this time hysterical with fear, he threw the hand into the fire and hid himself beneath the covers.

The laird did not appear downstairs the next morning. After some time Lady Margaret sent servants up to wake him. Not a sound came from the laird's bedroom in spite of the servants' repeated knocking and calling. His door was locked, and they had to break it down to gain entry. When they finally managed to enter the room, they found the laird lying on the floor. He was dead. His face, far from appearing peaceful, had a look of unimaginable terror. His neck was bruised, and the bruises appeared to be the marks of fingers around the laird's neck. He had been strangled by the hideous hand.

Meggernie Castle

The ghost of Meggernie Castle in Perthshire seems quite unperturbed by her unusual appearance and is quite willing, it would appear, not only to appear to the living but also to flirt with them.

The room in the castle where the ghost has been witnessed is now known as the Haunted Room, and on more than one occasion, men who have been sleeping in the room have been woken by the sensation of being kissed on the cheek. Those who see the ghost are said to see either her top half or her bottom half but never both together. The ghost is believed to be that of the wife of one of the chiefs of the Menzies clan. Her husband was profoundly jealous of the attentions that she attracted from other men and was forever accusing her of being unfaithful. His jealousy boiled over into uncontrollable rage one night, and he killed her. In order to dispose of the body, he cut it in half. He buried the top half of his wife in the tower and the bottom half in the churchyard. He then went abroad and on his return claimed that his wife had been with him but had died.

It is said that the bottom half of the unfortunate woman parades around the lower floors of the castle and the grounds outside. The top half, meanwhile, stays upstairs and persists in teasing sleeping guests with ghostly kisses.

Muchalls Castle

Scotland has a rich history of smuggling. Various places along its coastline were used in days gone by for the landing and concealment of contraband. Smuggling was not an activity confined to the lower classes. People from all walks of life succumbed to the temptation of avoiding the dreaded Exciseman.

Muchalls Castle, by Stonehaven, had a tunnel that was a godsend to smugglers. It led underground from the castle to the shore and was used for storing wine and spirits and as a secret means of coming and going for all those who might need it.

The cave at the far end of the tunnel was flooded at high tide, and it was here that a young lady of the family at Muchalls met her death. She had gone down the smugglers' tunnel for an assignation with her sweetheart, who would be arriving by boat, but fell into the sea at the end of the tunnel and drowned.

The ghost of the young woman is reputed to haunt one of the rooms in the castle. Like so many female ghosts, the figure of the young woman is green in colour.

Newton Castle

Newton Castle, Blairgowrie, dates from the fourteenth century and is haunted by the ghost of 'Lady Jean'. Her story is well known. She was Lady Jean Drummond, and she fell desperately in love with a local laird. He had dallied with her for a while but had become distracted by another woman. In order to win back the affection of her beloved, Lady Jean did her very best to make herself attractive. She dressed in finest silks and satins, wore shoes with silver buckles and adorned her braided hair with pearls and precious stones. The transformation in her appearance, however, was not enough to bring the heartless scoundrel back. She took to spending her time singing mournful songs of lost love as she sat alone in a tower of the castle.

Eventually she sought the advice of a local witch. The witch told her that her fine clothes were no good. She must dress in 'the witchin' claith o' green'. In order to do this, she must cut some grass from the churchyard, take a branch of a rowan tree from the gallows-knowe and bind them together with a plaited reed. Then she was to take them as darkness was falling to the Corbie Stone by the Cobble pool and sit there and wait.

This the Lady Jean did. After waiting for some time, she became aware of the sound of laughter. She could feel a strange sensation, as if something was pulling at her clothes. She fell asleep, and when she awoke at dawn she was dressed all in green.

The magic of the witch had worked, for Jean married her great love, Lord Ronald, still wearing the 'witchin' claith'. Her new husband was quite besotted with his bride in her strange green dress. The wedding ceremony had hardly taken place, however, than disaster struck. Lord Ronald looked at his bride and saw that something was far wrong. He took her hand in his, but it felt deathly cold. Then, to his horror, Jean let out an unearthly scream, fell to the ground and died. Her lifeless body was laid out on the bed where the wedding couple were to have consummated the marriage.

Lady Jean was buried nearby, and her gravestone is said to turn round three times each Halloween. Then the sound of her sad singing comes wafting from the tower at Newton Castle.

Sanquhar Castle

Sanquhar Castle, once home of the Crichtons of Dumfries, stands in ruins now but remains the haunt of the ghost of a man called John Wilson. John Wilson was the innocent party in a dispute that was going on in the late 1590s between Sir Thomas Kirkpatrick, John's master, and Douglas of Drumlanrig, ally of Robert Crichton, Lord of Sanquhar and Sheriff of Nithsdale. As an act of sheer spite against Wilson's master, Crichton had John Wilson locked up in jail, falsely accused of certain crimes. When Sir Thomas Kirkpatrick tried to protest Wilson's innocence, Crichton retaliated by having Wilson hanged. Wilson's ghost, groaning and rattling its chains, haunts the ruins of Sanquhar Castle as a testament of its one-time owner's barbarism and cruelty.

A second, female ghost is also said to haunt Sanquhar. She is a white lady, with long, pale tresses, quite beautiful to behold, so they say. Nobody is certain as to the identity of the White Lady, although she is possibly the ghost of Marion of Dalpeddar, who disappeared suspiciously in the 1590s and was thought perhaps to have befallen an unfortunate fate at the hands of Robert Crichton. In the 1870s, excavations around the castle uncovered the remains of a woman buried in a pit. The skeleton still had some hair attached to the skull. The hair was long and blond. Was this the skeleton of the White Lady of Sanquhar Castle?

Spedlins Tower

Spedlins Tower in Dumfriesshire was once upon a time haunted by a particularly hungry ghost.

At the end of the seventeenth century, Spedlins was the property of Sir Alexander Jardine, brother-in-law of the first Duke of Queensberry, William Douglas.

One of the laird's tenants, a miller by the name of Dunty Porteous, fell out of favour with his master. The laird, having right of pit and gallows, apprehended Porteous and took him to Spedlins. Porteous was locked in the dungeon of the tower to await judgment and suitable punishment for his misdemeanours. It was a grim place to sit and ponder one's fate – an underground pit with no light source. The only access to the dungeon was through a trapdoor. No sooner had Dunty Porteous been put away than Sir Alexander had to leave Spedlins to attend to some business in the capital city. He would have to deal with Dunty on his return.

Unfortunately, when the laird set off for Edinburgh, he took the key of the dungeon with him. In his absence, it would appear that either Dunty was forgotten about or nobody thought to break down the door of the dungeon and come to his aid. Whatever was the case, Dunty was abandoned, with tragic consequences.

Some time later, when Sir Alexander finally returned to Spedlins and the dungeon was unlocked, Dunty was found to have died of starvation. It is said that in the agonies of his dreadful hunger, the poor prisoner had chewed at his own hands. Any regret that Sir

Alexander felt for what had happened was clearly not great enough, for as soon as the spirit of Dunty Porteous was released from the confines of the dreadful dungeon it started to run riot at Spedlins.

Dunty's ghost was persistent and troublesome, running through Spedlins Tower screaming out in pain and hunger, crying for mercy and food. The spirit would give no peace to the Jardine family. Eventually, a chaplain was summoned to try to exorcise the ghost. His efforts were not entirely successful, for the ghost would not go away. Nevertheless, after a concerted effort, the minister and the family were able to confine Dunty's raging spirit to the dungeon with the help of a bible that was left at the site.

In time the binding of the bible became worn and needed to be repaired, so it was sent to Edinburgh to be rebound. No sooner had the bible left the premises than Dunty's ghost was on the loose again, tormenting the laird and his family as before. The bible had to be repaired and returned with all possible haste in order to confine the ghost once again.

The Jardine family eventually moved from Spedlins. The ghost of Dunty followed them, but the bible was moved too and Dunty remained subdued.

Tioram Castle

Tioram Castle has been uninhabited for more than two centuries, but the ruins that remain are sufficient to indicate to the visitor that it was indeed an impressive sight in its heyday, standing in spectacular surroundings, high on a rock overlooking the sea in north Argyll. It was a seat of the MacDonalds of Clanranald and had a colourful warfaring history.

The twelfth chief of Clanranald was John, who succeeded to his title in the late 1670s. He was a violent man, given to outbursts of temper with a distinctly sadistic touch, by all accounts. It is John, rather than his ancestral home, with which this story is concerned, for it was the man rather than his castle that was haunted. Perhaps it was because of all the wrongs he had done, which was certainly what most people suspected, but the reason does not really matter. John was haunted, not by a green lady or the spectre of one of the victims of his many cruelties. He was haunted by a frog – a hideous black creature of demonic proportions.

It is remarkable how close this story comes to the fairy tale of the princess and the frog. Just as the princess in the fairy tale was pursued relentlessly by her frog, so John found that he was unable to shake off his own slimy follower. If he left it locked in a room, it found its way out and appeared beside him again. If he tried to ride away, the frog would appear alongside him in the saddle. The frog was always there, whatever he was doing, whether he was asleep or awake. On one occasion, John tried to sail away from the castle, only to find the frog swimming alongside the boat. When he refused to let the frog on board, the weather turned so bad that all the people in the boat thought they might drown. John reluctantly let the frog on to the boat, whereupon, it is said, the weather turned calm once more almost instantly.

Perhaps if John had kissed the frog, as the princess in the fairy tale did, he might have found that it turned into something altogether more desirable, but he did not and his frog did not turn into anything else. The hideous creature remained with him, a constant but unwelcome companion, to the end of his days.

Other Haunted Castles

The stories of the castles in this chapter are just a taste of the hundreds of stories that the ancient fortifications of Scotland have to tell. They are some of the better known ones, but they are not necessarily the most intriguing to the eager ghost-hunter and others with interests in all things supernatural. Other castles that are said to be haunted make a long list indeed, but among them are the following:

Ardvreck Castle – the ghost of a former Lady of Ardvreck.

Balcomie Castle – the ghost of a young boy locked in a dungeon and starved to death.

Borthwick Castle – the ghost of Mary Queen of Scots and the ghost of a young girl impregnated and then murdered by Lord Borthwick.

Brodick Castle – the ghost of an unknown man and the ghost of a deer.

Buchanan Castle – anonymous groans.

Culzean Castle – a ghostly piper and a woman in a ball gown.

Duchal Castle – the ghost of an excommunicated monk.

Duns Castle – the ghost of a young soldier.

Inveraray Castle – the ghost of a murdered servant boy.

Kellie Castle – the ghost of Anne Erskine, who fell from an upper storey window.

Megginch Castle – the ghosts of two chattering old ladies.

Neidpath Castle – a white lady.

Newark Castle – the ghosts of women and children slaughtered by Covenanting forces.

Skibo Castle – the ghost of a girl lured to the castle by a servant and murdered by him.

Wemyss Castle – a green lady.

RELIGIOUS HAUNTS

Ruined cathedrals, dark corners of country churches, abbeys and priories can all quite easily take on a haunted appearance. Vaults, crypts and graveyards are full of the secrets of the dead. Hooded monks look like ghosts as they glide soundlessly along shadowy corridors. Members of the clergy, servants of God, are constantly engaged in the fight against sin, and hence the devil. It is only to be expected, therefore, that there are numerous stories of ghosts that torment members of the clergy, spirits that frequent religious meeting places and spectres that lurk in sacred burial places. Some of the stories are undoubtedly fictitious. Others, however, merit closer consideration, especially when the ghost is thought to be that of a real figure in history and when the presence of a spirit has been witnessed independently by more than one person, previously unaware of its supposed existence.

Dalarossie

Sundays in most parts of Scotland in modern times are days when families can choose to do more or less as they wish. Shopping in one of the many big shopping centres that have grown up around the major towns is a popular pastime, while other people may choose to spend the day catching up on do-it-yourself activities or working in the garden. Sports centres and swimming pools are open, and there are Sunday leagues for amateur sports of various kinds. For those who wish to spend the day in a more relaxed fashion, there are plenty of restaurants, pubs and hotels around the country where a leisurely lunch and a few glasses of wine can be enjoyed.

All this is a far cry from the days when the Sabbath in Scotland was a day reserved strictly for God and for rest. There are some parts of Scotland where the Sabbath is still observed to some degree and where some of the above pastimes are frowned upon, but even in those places the restrictions upon the activities of the God-fearing are considerably fewer than in days of old.

In times gone by it was unthinkable to venture from home for any other reason than to go to church. Children were not allowed out to play and no one was supposed to work. For women, the Sabbath must have brought quite a welcome break from cooking and cleaning. Sport was taboo on the Sabbath, as were playing cards, gambling and drinking. To break the laws of the Sabbath was believed to invite all sorts of terrible retribution.

There are quite a few stories about people who break the Sabbath – cautionary tales to warn others of the consequences of succumbing to temptation. Some appear elsewhere in this book – the story of Beardie of Glamis Castle, for example, in the previous chapter Page 71), and the story of the fisherman at Kylesku in Hotels and Public Houses (page 129). This story does not concern one individual, however, but a whole team of sportsmen.

Twenty miles or so from Inverness stands the parish church of Dalarossie, and just beside the parish church is the glebe, a patch of land that was used in times gone by as an area of recreation.

The story tells us that two families, the Shaws of Strathnairn and the Mackintoshes of Strathdearn, had arranged to have a game of shinty on the glebe on Christmas Day. When the game was first suggested, the Mackintoshes willingly agreed, but then they found out that Christmas Day was to fall on the Sabbath that year and decided to call the whole thing off. When their opponents turned up, all ready to play, they found that the Mackintoshes were not coming after all. The Shaws, however, were not quite so easily put off. There were enough people present to form two teams amongst themselves, so they divided up and played a game regardless. The game was a great success, and it was thought that no harm had come as a result of their breaking the Sabbath.

It seems they were tragically mistaken, for it is said that during the course of the following year every man who had played on that day died.

The ghostly shinty players return to Dalarossie once a year. Every Christmas, they play their game on the glebe as they did all those years ago on that fateful Sabbath.

Durness

In Durness in Sutherland a story is told of a manse that was haunted by a particularly ominous spirit.

According to the legend, the spirit first manifested itself many years ago when the minister in Durness became aware of the sound of knocking at his front door. The knocking became a regular occurrence. As the minister never heard anyone approaching the door, he was suspicious and did not answer the knocks.

After several repetitions of the strange phenomenon, the minister invited a colleague, the minister from Kinlochbervie, to call on him one night. He did not give the reason for his invitation. The minister from Kinlochbervie duly made the journey to Durness and settled down for a pleasant evening. After some time had passed, the men heard a knocking at the front door. The Durness minister asked his friend if he would answer it, and his friend obliged, having no idea that the knocking meant anything sinister.

The Kinlochbervie minister cheerfully went and opened the door, only to be faced with the fearful apparition of an old man wrapped in a shroud. Terrified, he saddled his horse at once and rode back to Kinlochbervie with all possible speed. He had not escaped the clutches of the terrible death spirit, however. It is said that barely a month later, although he was a man of robust health and only in his mid-forties, the Kinlochbervie minister died suddenly and mysteriously. The tragedy became a double one when his wife followed him to the grave very shortly afterwards.

It seems unfair that the minister from Durness should survive unscathed after such cowardly behaviour on his own part, but it would appear that the deathly figure that came to his door had no sense of justice. It seemed, rather, to want to take whomever it could.

Lairg

At the end of the eighteenth century there lived in Lairg in Sutherland a mildly eccentric minister. In spite of being a humble clergyman, the Reverend Thomas Mackay is said to have dressed in much grander ecclesiastical attire. He died early in the 1800s, and the manse was thereafter occupied by ministers with more sober habits of dress.

The minister who lived in the manse in 1826 had two daughters, and it was they who saw the ghost for the first time. They heard a knock at the front door and went to answer it. When they opened the door they saw an old man standing on the doorstep, dressed in a long black robe. He said nothing but peered into the house for a few moments before turning away from the girls and walking off. The girls thought that the visitor might be looking for their father, so they ran to find him. When their father came to greet the visitor, there was no sign of the old man, either at the door or in the surrounding area. It seemed as if he had vanished completely.

When the family told some other older parishioners about their strange old visitor and described his appearance and attire, the parishioners were able to enlighten them as to their visitor's identity. It was none other than the Reverend Thomas Mackay, paying a visit to his former home.

The manse is no longer there; it fell into disrepair and became a ruin. However, the Reverend Thomas Mackay is said to pop back from time to time to visit the site where it once stood. It is said that one night his appearance stopped the activities of two poachers in the neighbourhood. When they heard strange noises coming from the vicinity of the former manse they abandoned all ideas of a profitable night's work and fled.

Melrose Abbey

The ruins of Melrose Abbey are believed to be the haunt of a rather more sinister ghost than some. Several people have reported noticing a strange chill in the atmosphere near the place where a man called Michael Scott was buried in the late thirteenth century.

Michael Scott was a very intelligent man of great learning, interested in philosophy and science. During his lifetime he acquired a reputation as a practitioner of the black arts, and he was said to possess strange supernatural powers. It may have been the case that he was simply rather a scary intellectual, whose brain and knowledge seemed threatening to other less educated or intelligent people. Nonetheless, he was a man who inspired fear among many people, both in life and after death. The site of his grave in the abbey is believed to be haunted by his spirit. The sensations that are felt by those who are sensitive to such things are not pleasant ones. Many people reportedly have felt an ominous chill in the air when they have stood in the vicinity.

Stories of vampirism and other crimes, sometimes attributed to Michael Scott, sometimes to a monk who fell from grace in ancient times, are also associated with Melrose Abbey. A ghostly figure that has been reportedly seen sliding like a snake along the ground in the Abbey ruins is taken to be a manifestation of this spirit.

Iona

The tiny island of Iona off the west coast of Scotland is visited by many hundreds of people every year. It is a place of historical interest and pilgrimage, and it was here that St Columba landed from Ireland to begin his mission of spreading the word of God in Scotland in the sixth century. Kings of Scotland from ancient times are buried on Iona, and today the island is a religious centre of quite considerable significance.

Iona was attacked by the Vikings on several occasions in times gone by, and the monastery of St Columba had to be restored repeatedly. The ghostly forms of Viking longboats are still said to visit the island from time to time. The ships glide into the harbour by night and eerie figures scramble ashore, re-enacting over and over again their desecration of this sacred place.

Monks have been reported as having been seen at various places on the island, especially in the area of the monastery, and the sound of their chanting has also been heard on several occasions.

Perth

In the early years of the nineteenth century, an Edinburgh priest who had moved to Perth, called Father McKay, was approached by a woman who had been troubled for some time by a conscience-stricken ghost. The problem was solved without the need for exorcism or dramatic intervention of any kind.

Anne Simpson, the woman who sought Father McKay's assistance, was not of the Catholic faith, but she had good reason for asking the help of a Catholic priest. It turned out that the ghost that had been appearing to her night after night was that of a woman whom she had known as a familiar figure around the army barracks nearby. The woman's name was Molloy, and she had worked in the barracks laundry. Mrs Molloy's ghost, when it appeared to Anne Simpson, was most persistent. Mrs Molloy owed money – three shillings and ten pence. She wanted Anne Simpson to tell a priest and ask him to set matters right.

So here was Anne Simpson, tired of constantly interrupted sleep, doing the bidding of a ghost! Lesser men might have sent the poor woman away and told her to stop talking such nonsense, but Father McKay listened to her story patiently and assured her that he would see what he could do.

He made enquiries at the barracks first of all. Sure enough, there had been a woman called Molloy working there, but she had died some time before. Had she owed any money to anybody in the barracks, the priest wanted to know. No, she had not owed any money there. The priest had to take his search a little farther afield. Visiting local traders, he found himself in the grocer's shop. When he asked about Mrs Molloy, he discovered that when she had died she was in debt to the grocer. And the amount of the debt? Three shillings and ten pence exactly.

The kindly priest settled the outstanding amount and left the shop. When he saw Anne Simpson some days later, he asked whether Mrs Molloy's ghost had appeared to her recently. He was quite relieved to hear that the ghost seemed to have gone. Obviously the spirit of Mrs Molloy felt at peace now that she had got all her affairs in order!

Rosslyn Chapel

Rosslyn Chapel lies quite close to Edinburgh, to the south of the city. Founded in 1446 by William Sinclair, Earl of Orkney, it is a popular visitor site and a place of historical, religious and architectural interest.

Historically, the chapel is the subject of much controversy. Some historians believe that the chapel had strong links in the past with the Knights Templar. Many theories have been proposed as to the supposed existence of religious relics – some believe this includes the Holy Grail – hidden within an underground vault beneath the floor of the chapel. The most recent theory at the time of writing is the most astonishing – that the chapel has buried beneath it the mummified head of Christ, which was worshipped by the Knights Templar hundreds of years ago. The trustees of the chapel are under constant pressure to carry out excavations to find out whether there is any truth in any of the many theories about its mysterious past.

Architecturally, Rosslyn is interesting for several different reasons. The interior of the chapel is unusually ornate for a Scottish church and is unique amongst its contemporaries. Scottish religious buildings of the time were characteristically very plain in design, and although Rosslyn is essentially a Gothic building, its fanciful decoration and exotic – some would say eccentric – ornament make it stand apart from all others. There is evidence to suggest that many foreign craftsmen were employed in its construction, which would account in part for some of the decorative elements that are in evidence in the building. One piece of particular merit within the chapel is a very ornate and beautifully carved pillar known as the Apprentice or Prentice Pillar. The Apprentice Pillar has a story of its own to tell. The story goes that when the chapel was being constructed a stone mason was requested to carve this pillar in the style of a particular column in Rome. The mason was finding it difficult to reproduce the desired effect using the picture he had of the column as his only source of inspiration. To prepare himself adequately for the task, he decided to travel to Rome to see the original column for himself. A journey of this sort was quite an undertaking in those days, and the mason was away for some weeks. In the absence of his master, the stonemason's apprentice, who had been left behind, decided to try to carve a pillar himself. He studied the picture that his master had been given and set to work.

When the stonemason returned from Italy, he found that the work that his apprentice had done was far superior to anything he might have been able to carve himself. In a fit of rage and jealousy, he killed his apprentice on the spot. The story of the murder is given credence by the fact that there had to be a delay between the construction of the chapel and its eventual consecration, which took place only after an Act of Reconciliation had been sought from the Archbishop of St Andrews.

The ghostly apprentice returned to haunt the chapel and the work of which he was so proud. His mournful figure has been seen standing beside his pillar and the sound of his weeping has been heard by many people who have visited the chapel over the years.

Another ghostly figure that frequents the chapel and its surroundings is the figure of a monk clad in grey. He has appeared to visitors on quite a few occasions, both inside and outside the chapel.

St Andrews Cathedral

St Andrews Cathedral, dating from the twelfth century, lies in ruins now but was once the largest cathedral in Scotland and a powerful and influential religious centre. In all, building work took almost two hundred years. The royal burgh of St Andrews, in which the cathedral stands, is a very old and beautiful university town, of great interest both to the historian and the ghost-hunter.

The cathedral has two ghosts that are particularly well known, one a woman, the other a man.

In the grounds of the cathedral at St Andrews is St Rule's Tower, a remnant of St Rule's Church, which was built before the cathedral and used to hold the relics of St Andrew. It is here that the male ghost has been seen. The tower is quite high, and the view from the top, looking over the town, is well worth seeing, so it is quite a popular visiting place. One visitor to the tower several years ago was startled by a figure in a cassock who appeared as he was climbing to the top. The tourist missed his footing on one of the steps and stumbled. Far from wishing to frighten the tourist, the cowled figure had genuinely intended to be helpful, for the tourist heard him offer to give him his arm on the way up the stairs. The tourist, swiftly recovering his balance, refused politely, and the figure stepped to one side to allow him to pass and then vanished without trace.

When the tourist came out of the tower at the end of his visit, he asked the man at the door whether anyone else had been in the tower at the same time as himself. The man at the door said that there had been no one else there, but he knew who, or what, the tourist had seen. The tourist discovered that the figure that he had seen was well known to those who knew the tower. He was a monk who would appear from time to time at St Rule's – not a malevolent spirit at all, it would seem, but a kindly ghost who liked to make sure that visitors made their way safely to the top of the spiral staircase.

The female ghost is a white lady who has been seen in the grounds of the cathedral. The ghost was observed to be wearing white gloves. Some of the sightings may well have been fanciful, perhaps fuelled by alcohol, as they were made by students returning from late-night revelries. Nevertheless, the White Lady has also been seen by more sober citizens of the town from time to time over a period of nearly two centuries.

The identity of the White Lady is not known, but it may be that her burial place is very near. In 1868, historians investigating the tower opened a sealed vault there and discovered it to be a burial place. There were six or so coffins inside it. They also found, it is claimed, the mummified body of a young woman wearing white gloves. The vault was re-sealed, but it appears that the historians had discovered part of the answer to the mysterious appearances of the White Lady of St Andrews.

Sanquhar Kirkyard

In the eighteenth and nineteenth centuries, the kirkyard at Sanquhar, in the Borders, achieved notoriety on account of the ghostly activities of a man called Abraham Crichton. Abraham Crichton died in 1745 in a particularly unpleasant manner after a colourful life.

Crichton was a wealthy man, laird of Carco and the owner of several properties in the area as well as a great deal of land. However, much to the suspicion of various local people, he was declared bankrupt in 1741. His properties and land were sold off bit by bit, but rumours were circulated that Crichton was not in the dire straits that he would have people believe. He had, somewhere, secreted away a great deal of money. This, combined with the manner of his death, made it hardly surprising that his tortured soul would be unable to find peace.

There was a disused church in the district, which had been the kirk of a former parish, that of Kirkbride. For some years there had been a dispute as to what to do with the building. Some locals wanted to tear it down, whilst in the opinion of others such an act amounted to sacrilege. The story goes that previous attempts to demolish the church had been unsuccessful and that those who had taken part in the exercise found themselves the victims of considerable misfortune as a result. In the eyes of those who believed in such things, these happenings had been manifestations of the wrath of God.

Abraham Crichton was having none of this. He wanted the church to be brought down. He engaged a group of workmen to accompany him to the building to start demolition. They set to work, but hardly had they done so than an almighty storm blew up, preventing them from getting any work done. Forced to abandon their efforts until the next day, they all set off for home.

Whilst riding back from Kirkbride, Abraham Crichton met with disaster. A bolt of lightning caused his horse to rear up in panic and Crichton was unseated. A tumble from a horse is bad enough, but one of Crichton's feet had become wedged in the stirrup and as the horse bolted, he was dragged along in its wake. The horse galloped off at a great rate, and it did not stop, nor even slow down, until it reached Dalpeddar. When the frightened beast finally drew to a halt, its owner lay by its side, lifeless and bloody.

It seemed as if the death of Abraham Crichton was divine retribution. Not only had this man been dishonest in his financial dealings, said his critics, but he had also been guilty of sacrilege. He should never have tried to tear the church down. The locals shook their heads and tut-tutted self-righteously as preparations were made for Crichton's funeral.

They had not seen the last of Abraham Crichton, however. Not long after he was buried in the graveyard at Sanquhar, he returned in ghostly form. The ghost of Abraham Crichton caused great consternation in the district. He would pursue passers-by in the fields next to the churchyard. He would appear suddenly in the churchyard itself, frightening the life out of anyone who happened to be there. Always, he seemed to be trying to speak to those whom he followed. His hand would stretch out in entreaty, but none dared to take it. The kirkyard at Sanquhar became a place much feared in the hours of darkness. Locals would take detours in order to avoid passing close to the church as a longer walk was considered well worth the effort if it meant avoiding the ghost of Abraham Crichton. News of the haunting spread, and Sanquhar became a topic of heated debate amongst those who had any interest in matters paranormal.

At length it was decided that something had to be done, the ghost was causing too many difficulties. A minister by the name of Hunter was appointed to deal with Crichton's troublesome spirit. The bold minister took himself to the kirkyard one dark night with a bible and a sword to await an encounter with Crichton. He insisted on carrying out his vigil alone, and no one saw what came to pass in the course of the night. When morning came, however, the minister left the churchyard, tired but in confident mood. He never related precisely what happened during those long hours of darkness. He was, however, able to give his assurance that Abraham Crichton's ghost would wander no more.

The ghost was never seen after that, but, just in case, the people of Sanquhar secured his tombstone in its place over the grave with very sturdy chains.

GHOSTS IN THE HOUSE

It is not only buildings of great history or particular architectural interest that feel the chill of the ghost's presence. Homes all over Scotland, both old and relatively new, are claimed to have been the site of supernatural occurrences. Some of these claims will certainly be fanciful, some will be mere sensationalism, but many are simply too strange to be ignored.

Abbotsford House, Melrose

Abbotsford House was the home of the celebrated poet and novelist Sir Walter Scott and is now a popular tourist attraction. A great deal of building work was carried out there according to Scott's own specifications, incorporating many of the features he had seen and admired in various buildings he had visited throughout Scotland during his life.

The house must have been a considerable financial burden to the novelist, especially after he suffered great losses when the publisher's firm in which he was a partner collapsed, but Scott worked at his writing with incredible industry to keep the house in his possession and to pay off his debts before his death. Before he died, Sir Walter Scott is reported to have made claims that the house was haunted, the ghost being, it was thought, that of one of the craftsmen who had worked on the building, a man named George Bullock. George Bullock had had a supervisory role in many of the building works at Abbotsford, but he died while the work was still in progress.

Since the death of Sir Walter Scott himself at Abbotsford in 1832, there have been stories of the writer putting in an appearance from time to time in ghostly form, often in the dining room in which he spent his last days and where he eventually died.

Allanbank House, Berwickshire

Allanbank House is now no longer standing, having been destroyed in the early nineteenth century, but the ghost that once frequented the house is well remembered. She is known as 'Pearlin' Jean' – the word 'Pearlin'' referring to the distinct pattern of the lace that she wore on her collar and dress. She was thought to have been the lover of the first baronet of Allanbank, Robert Stuart, who lived in the seventeenth century.

According to some versions of the story, Jean was French and lived as a nun (presumably not in a closed convent) until she met Robert Stuart and became his lover. Some say that Pearlin' Jean actually returned to Scotland and to Allanbank with Stuart for a while. Whether or not this was the case, it appeared that Stuart did not see her as a suitable wife and, in time, he became engaged to another woman, leaving poor Jean in the lurch. Jean had sacrificed everything to be with Robert: her love, her respectability – virtually her life. She could not return to her former life; she had nothing more to lose.

Some versions of the story say that what happened next took place in Paris, whilst others place the incident at Allanbank itself. Wherever it happened, the consequences were tragic. Robert Stuart was driving out in his coach when the figure of Pearlin' Jean appeared in front of the carriage. She jumped up on to the carriage with the intention of confronting Robert and making him change his mind. Robert, on the other hand, was horrified to see Jean. He whipped the horses into a gallop, causing the carriage to move forward with a great jolt. Jean lost her grip and was thrown from her perch, falling under the wheels of the carriage. Whether by accident or by design, Robert saw his former sweetheart crushed to death beneath the wheels as the horses galloped on.

It was Robert himself who first saw the ghost of Pearlin' Jean. He was returning to Allanbank one night when he saw her, a ghostly white figure perched at the gateway, her head covered in blood. He was rendered speechless with fear.

Pearlin' Jean continued to shatter the peace of the house long after her death, banging doors and clattering around the corridors. She was still seen and heard at Allanbank long after the death of Robert Stuart, but future inhabitants of the house were not threatened by her presence as he had been. She became a familiar sight and sound, regarded with something approaching affection. Visitors, however, were often startled by her antics and her bloody appearance.

Since the destruction of the house, Pearlin' Jean seems to have gone, but she will be long remembered.

Ballachulish House, Argyll

Ballachulish House has more than one ghost, but one particular tale informs us that a 'living ghost' once made a habit of visiting the place.

The house was at one time occupied by the family of Sir Harold Boulton. Many years before he moved into Ballachulish House, Sir Harold had heard his mother talk of a recurrent dream she had had of visiting a beautiful house set amidst spectacular scenery. In her dreams she had become acquainted with every corner of the place, much as if she had really been there.

Several years later, Mrs Boulton, by then quite elderly, visited Ballachulish House for the first time before her son and his family had moved in. The house was at that time owned by Lady Beresford. Mrs Boulton found to her great surprise that she already knew the house very well indeed – it was the house with which she had become intimately acquainted in her dreams.

When Mrs Boulton spoke to Lady Beresford about this, giving credence to her story with additional knowledge about structural alterations that had taken place over the years, she was pleased to see that Lady Beresford took her quite seriously. Ballachulish House had been visited several times over the years by the benign spectre of a lady. Now, Lady Beresford was quite convinced that the spectre was in fact the living ghost of Mrs Boulton.

Ballechin House, Perthshire

Ballechin House used to stand near Dunkeld, some miles from Perth. It was built at the beginning of the nineteenth century and was the home of the Steuart family. Strange goings-on at Ballechin House are said to have started after the death of Major Robert Steuart in 1876. The house was inherited by John Steuart, the major's nephew.

In the late 1890s the house was rented out for a period of some months. The family that had taken the lease, however, stayed no more than a matter of weeks. They left Ballechin in fear, having been tormented by a cacophony of strange sounds: bumps, rattles, thumps and knocks, doors slamming, footsteps and angry voices. They had also experienced an unnatural chill about the building.

On another occasion, a guest in the house was continuously tormented by disturbing noises. One night he reported that he had woken to hear what sounded like a dog trying to burst into his room. The house became the focus of great curiosity, and several people with an interest in psychical research visited the place or stayed there for a while over the course of time in an attempt to investigate further the cause of the strange events that were supposed to be happening there.

Ballechin was also haunted by nuns, who could be seen outside the house. John Steuart himself was witness to this sight and to the sounds of loud knocking. John was killed by a cab in London, and it is said that he was given some warning of his untimely death by the ghostly sights and sounds at Ballechin.

Blythswood Square, Glasgow

Blythswood Square in the centre of Glasgow is a square of fine Georgian buildings with a mixed history. Now the site of offices of lawyers and accountants, it once had a reputation as being something of a red-light district. In years before that, it was more of a residential area and considered to be a very desirable place to live.

One particular gentleman, house-hunting in the area, came upon a house in Blythswood Square that was for sale. Upon inspecting the property, he was very impressed with it all, with the exception of the bathroom. There was something about the bathroom that gave the house a very unpleasant air, and the gentleman could not quite put his finger on what it was. The room had a cold and dreary atmosphere, but there was something else, something foreboding. The room made him shudder. Nevertheless, the thought of having a prestigious address such as this was too tempting for both the gentleman and his wife. The bathroom would surely take on a brighter atmosphere with a few coats of fresh paint and new fittings. They bought the house and moved in.

The gentleman still felt very uneasy about using the bathroom, in spite of its bright new appearance and in spite of his family's reassurances that all was normal. He did not like to close the door when he was having a bath. His wife, however, protested at such immodest behaviour. Reluctantly, the gentleman had to respect her wishes. The next time he went to take a bath, he summoned up the courage to close the door behind him.

The gentleman could see that there was no one else in the bathroom, but in spite of this he still had the distinct feeling that there was someone else there. It was uncanny. Trying to ignore his feelings of misgiving, he placed his candle at the edge of the bath, undressed and stepped into the water.

Hardly had the gentleman got into the bath, however, than he heard strange sounds coming from the fire grate. He tried to ignore them but they persisted. He got up to investigate, his heart hammering. Cautiously he stepped out of the bath. Suddenly the candle went out, and as the room was plunged into darkness, the gentleman tripped and fell to the floor. Frozen with terror, he then heard the sounds of loud splashing coming from the bath. Someone was in the bath, washing! But that was impossible – there was nobody there!

The gentleman hardly had time to ponder upon this, for after only a few seconds he heard the cupboard door behind him opening. A figure stepped out of the cupboard. The gentleman could hear the rustling of skirts and smell the cloying scent of perfume. The gentleman had no time to get out of the ghostly figure's way. A chilly foot in a high-heeled shoe stepped on his back quite carelessly as the spectre of a woman, apparently oblivious of the gentleman's presence, made her way towards the bath.

The gentleman gasped and listened. Sounds of a struggle came from the bath, a violent struggle. There was much splashing and thrashing about. Then, all of a sudden, the noises stopped. The woman turned to face the gentleman, and through the darkness he saw a ghostly white face quite startling in its luminosity. The face was obviously that of a beautiful woman, but it was contorted with an expression of pure hatred.

The gentleman had seen and heard enough. He fumbled his way to the bathroom door, unlocked it and fled to the safety of his bedroom. When he told his wife what had happened, he was met with ridicule and told not to be so foolish. His fear was dismissed as mere hysteria.

Then one morning the gentleman's son went to use the bathroom and was greeted with the sight of a dead man floating in the bath water. His screams alerted the rest of the family, who came running. When they went into the bathroom they could see nothing. But when they were coming out, they were all witness to the sight of a beautiful dark-haired woman, a look of unmistakable hatred on her face, sweeping past them into the bathroom cupboard.

The family left the house – no matter how desirable the address, the spectral inhabitants made life there unbearable. Once they had found themselves a suitable, less sinister place to live, they made enquiries about the history of the house in Blythswood Square.

Their investigations were quite enlightening. Apparently the house had once been the property of a wealthy man married to a Spanish woman with a violent temper. The man had been found drowned in his bath one morning. The circumstances had been suspicious, but no foul play could be proved, and his beautiful widow left the country.

The gentleman and his family knew the terrible truth about what had happened, and the gentleman now realised that what he had experienced was the ghostly re-enactment of the whole sordid affair.

Boleskin House, Inverness-shire

Boleskin House is situated on the southeast shores of Loch Ness, close to the village of Foyers. The house dates from the second half of the eighteenth century, and its history was unremarkable until it was bought just over a century later by a man called Aleister Crowley. Had Aleister Crowley lived three hundred years before, his activities would have had to have been conducted in the utmost secrecy or he would have surely met a premature and exceedingly unpleasant end. As it was, Mr Crowley took a certain pride in the fact that he was proclaimed to be the 'wickedest man in the world'. He was known to practise black magic and to be obsessed with the satanic and profane. His house was the scene of drug- and alcohol-fuelled orgies, sacrifice and satanic ritual. He died in 1947. Boleskin House is said to be troubled by evil spirits and poltergeist activity, and both the house and the graveyard nearby – rumoured to be connected by a secret underground tunnel – are said to be sites that witches haunt. The eerie atmosphere that surrounds the place and the knowledge of the lifestyle of its one-time occupant make this hardly surprising.

Broomhill House, Lanarkshire

The case of Broomhill House was given a great deal of publicity in the 1960s when a television documentary was made on the subject of its ghost. The house stood on a site that had been inhabited for hundreds of years, buildings of various forms having been successively built and destroyed during the course of time. The house in its final form was the home of the McNeil-Hamilton family at the turn of the century, and the last of the family to live there was

Captain Henry Montgomery McNeil-Hamilton. The ghost that haunts the ruins, the Black Lady, is well known to locals in Larkhall, the area of Lanarkshire where the ruins of the house stand. The house has attracted the interest of clairvoyants and ghost-hunters alike, and much research has been carried out by psychic investigators and other interested parties to find out who the Black Lady was and why she haunts the place.

The ghost is a sad one, it would appear, and she has been seen and has been making her presence felt since quite early on in the twentieth century.

Captain Henry McNeil-Hamilton was a military man and served in South Africa during the Boer War. It is thought that the Black Lady was in fact an Indian woman who, having been taken to South Africa, found herself working for the British Army there. She was possibly brought to Scotland by McNeil-Hamilton to live as his mistress. There are stories of such a lady living at Broomhill, who seemed to disappear in mysterious circumstances, and some people believe that she may have met a violent end.

Broomhill suffered from a fire in the 1940s and was badly damaged. The McNeil-Hamilton family sold the house and land in 1954. The house, already in a desperate state, fell further into ruin and very little remains now. Nevertheless, in spite of attempts at exorcism over the years, the Black Lady is still said to be there, her appearances characterised by an overpowering feeling of melancholy and a smell of spices and perfume.

Bruntsfield, Edinburgh

There was, until the beginning of the nineteenth century, a house by Bruntsfield Links, one of great age, having been built in the fourteenth century, and of considerable elegance. In the years leading up to its eventual demolition (after which a school was built on the site), the house was inhabited by Lieutenant-General Robertson of Lawers and his staff. Not long after he had taken up residence in the house, the general received a complaint from one of his servants that he was getting very little sleep on account of a headless woman, carrying a baby, who would appear near the fireplace in his room night after night. The complainant was known to have a tendency to indulge in strong drink whenever given the opportunity, so naturally the general assumed at first that his servant was suffering from alcohol-induced delusions. As time wore on, however, the servant persisted with his complaints and eventually left the house to look for work somewhere else.

The general thereafter had the room in which the servant had slept primarily used for storage. No one went into the room at night, so no more ghosts were seen.

The story might have been completely forgotten about had it not been for the fact that the building was subjected to a demolition order some years later. When the builders began to tear the building down, they lifted the hearth in the servant's old room and found the skeletal remains of a woman and a baby. The woman had had her head severed – a particularly brutal act of violence by any standards. The story goes that she must have been sewing when her killer took her by surprise, for scissors and a needle were found beside the bones of her hands, as if she had been holding them. Who she was and why she was killed so savagely along with her child, nobody will ever know.

Buckingham Terrace, Edinburgh

Buckingham Terrace is situated by the Dean Bridge, close to the centre of Edinburgh. It is an imposing crescent of houses, many of which are divided into elegant flats.

In the nineteenth century, the residents in one particular flat in Buckingham Terrace, the Gordon family, became aware of a sinister presence in their home shortly after moving in. The flat above had been uninhabited for some time and, apart from some pieces of furniture that were stored there, it was empty. Mrs Gordon was therefore very surprised and quite concerned when she awoke one night to hear noises coming from the room above her head. There was a great deal of banging and thumping, as if heavy objects were being moved around. The noises were repeated the next night, and Mrs Gordon was moved to make a complaint to the landlord. No satisfactory explanation could be offered for the disturbances, however. The Gordon family were the only occupants of the building. There was little the landlord could do except suggest that perhaps Mrs Gordon's ears were deceiving her and that the noise was travelling from farther away, perhaps the adjoining building.

Mrs Gordon was adamant. The noises were coming from the upper flat, from the room directly above her bedroom.

It was not long after this that Mrs Gordon began to become aware of a distinct feeling of dread when she was in her bedroom. She woke one night feeling quite fearful. Normally a calm, rational sort of person, she was not given to experiencing such feelings. It felt to her as if something or someone was in the room, although she could see nothing. The presence – for it now seemed certain that something was there – would move past her as she lay in bed at night, then go out of her room quietly. After it had left Mrs Gordon's room, she could hear it climbing the stairs to the floor above. The sounds, quiet at first, would then build to a sudden crescendo. The banging noises that she had heard on previous occasions would start up again. Then the sounds would change in quality once more, and Mrs Gordon would hear staccato, stamping noises, as if someone was jumping up and down on the floor above her head.

There was little Mrs Gordon could do about the strange occurrences, for any suggestion she might make to the landlord that the place might be haunted would undoubtedly have been met with denial and probably derision. She had enquired of the rest of her family whether they had been disturbed by anything at night, but they had not heard a thing.

Then Mrs Gordon's daughter experienced similar occurrences. Her mother was away, and she decided to sleep in her room one night. She had barely opened the door than she felt something push past her, moving towards the stair to the upper floor. The girl, perhaps emboldened by a rush of adrenaline, charged after the 'thing' as it headed for the empty flat above. At the doorway, she stopped, but she could hear that the thing had gone inside. Now, from the sounds she could hear through the door, the 'thing' was moving furniture around!

Tentatively the girl tried the door and found it to be unlocked. She turned the handle, pushed the door wide open and stared into the gloom from the doorway. Inside, she could just make out a dark figure bending over the open case of a grandfather clock. Something told her that the figure was not human or, at least, not a living human. Suddenly her courage deserted her, and she froze in terror. The figure turned towards her. She ran, as fast as her legs could carry her, back down to the safety of her own flat. When the girl told her mother about what had happened, Mrs Gordon's suspicions that the building was haunted grew even stronger.

The ghostly figure appeared once more, this time to Mrs Gordon. She was lying in her bed one night when she became aware of the (now familiar) feeling of dread again. She looked up and saw a man standing in the doorway of the bedroom. He had a sinister, distracted air about him. In his hands he held what looked like a bundle of rags.

The family had experienced quite enough. They arranged forthwith to leave the flat in Buckingham Terrace.

Once they had settled comfortably elsewhere, however, Mrs Gordon determined to see what she could find out about the history of their flat in Buckingham Terrace. Investigations revealed that she and her family were not the only ones to believe that the place was haunted. Several rumours circulated about the flat, one of which was the following, which Mrs Gordon took to be the most likely.

According to the story, a retired seaman, a former captain in the merchant navy, had lived in the Gordons' flat some time before. The man was an alcoholic and was also believed to have been mentally disturbed. There had been a family with a young baby living in the flat above at that time, and the baby, as babies do, often cried at night. On one particular night, the baby, who had been left alone for a while, had woken and was crying. The constant noise of the crying had annoyed the seaman to such an extent that he had stormed upstairs in a drunken rage and killed the baby. In a pathetic effort to conceal his crime, he had tried to hide the baby's body in the case of a grandfather clock. Of course, the dreadful deed had soon been discovered, and the seaman was eventually committed to an asylum, where it was said that he took his own life.

This story was dreadful indeed, but it did explain to the Gordon family why the presence kept thundering upstairs and why the ghostly figure had been bent over the open case of the grandfather clock. The seaman's ghost was condemned to re-enact his ghastly deed over and over again.

Crail, Fife

In the picturesque fishing town of Crail, in the East Neuk of Fife, a row of Victorian houses stands overlooking the harbour. They were built by a wealthy man for his five daughters, all spinsters. One of these houses has for several years been the holiday home of an Edinburgh family who have spent many a blissful summer walking the seaside paths and guddling about on the beach nearby. The house is now seeing its third generation of the family approach adulthood and must have many happy memories stored within its walls. Members of the family and visitors who have stayed in the house testify to the existence of a ghost in one of the bedrooms. The ghost is not a frightening one. All that can be seen through the darkness is a pair of eyes, which appear to be those of a woman. The eyes always appear in the same corner of the room, hidden from the window by a large wardrobe and out of reach of the reflection of any mirror or other trick of the light. The woman's eyes watch silently but benevolently. Perhaps the original occupant of the house, denied for whatever reason the pleasures of marriage and family life, takes some comfort from the fact that her old home is now frequented by families and children.

Crawford Priory, Fife

In spite of the ecclesiastical sound of the name of the place, Crawford Priory has no connections with the church whatsoever. It was built as a private home in 1813 by Lady Mary Crawford. Its architecture harks back to much earlier times, inspired as it is by Gothic religious style. On a gloomy day its impressive facade looks undeniably grim; in fact, it looks as if it ought to be haunted. The imaginative visitor could quite easily conjure up a picture of sinister cowled figures moving around the grounds or the headless spectre of some unfortunate figure from the past. Such a vision would certainly fit the appearance of the building but is far removed from the truth.

Crawford Priory is haunted, but the ghost is free of any malevolence or unhappy history. Lady Mary was an eccentric figure by all accounts, a determined and sometimes fierce spinster who, having indulged her fantasy in the building of Crawford Priory, chose to share her life with a menagerie of animals upon whom she doted. She kept many animals and birds, both wild and domestic, at the priory and seemed to prefer their company to that of human beings. Lady Mary demonstrated her great concern for their welfare even after her death. In her will, she left instructions regarding the euthanasia of her brother's horse, which she had been looking after. She wanted the beast to suffer as little pain and distress as possible.

Lady Mary Crawford died in 1833, and her funeral was quite an impressive affair. She is buried in the family mausoleum nearby, but her ghost remains at the priory, wandering around the grounds, beckoning her beloved creatures to come to her.

Cullen House, Banffshire

Cullen House is situated close to the fishing village of Cullen in Banffshire, on the northeast coast of Scotland. The house and its lands have been the property of the Earls of Seafield for more than two hundred years. The ghost that haunts Cullen House is thought to be that of the third Earl of Seafield, by the name of James

Ogilvie. James was known to suffer from a severely disabling form of mental illness and was often seized by fits of an uncontrollable nature, during which he was said to be a danger both to himself and to others. When one of these fits was imminent, his staff, who could recognise the signs, would do their best to secure him and keep him from harm. On one occasion, however, they were unsuccessful. The 'Mad Earl', as he was known, had a particularly violent attack, in the course of which there was a struggle between him and a very close friend. The friend was killed. When the Earl regained his wits and realised what he had done, he was completely overcome with despair and anguish. So distressed was he that he took his own life. His ghost is said to wander the site even now.

Dalkeith, Midlothian

An attractive old house on the edge of Dalkeith, just outside Edinburgh, was the scene of some very sinister events early in the twentieth century. On 3 February 1911, a large dinner party was held, after which several people fell dangerously ill and two lost their lives. A postmortem examination showed that they had been poisoned. The two dead men were named as John Hutchinson and Alec Clapperton. The poisoner turned out to have been John, the son of Charles Hutchinson. He fled to the Channel Islands after the incident and when finally cornered by police there, he ended his own life by taking prussic acid.

A strange presence, thought to be the ghost of Charles Hutchinson, remains very much in evidence in the house nowadays, in the room where the dinner party took place. The family who live there testify to a strange atmosphere in the room and the family dogs are reluctant to enter it.

Frendraught House, Aberdeenshire

Frendraught House, as it stands today, was constructed in the seventeenth century around a much older castle. The property stands in beautiful surroundings close to the town of Huntly and is haunted by a ghost whose story starts in 1630.

In 1630, the laird of Frendraught at the time, Sir James Crichton, killed Gordon of Rothiemay in a dispute over land. As a consequence of this, he was ordered by the Marquis of Huntly to pay compensation, or blood money, to Gordon's son and namesake.

Some time later, Crichton became involved in a feud with Leslie of Pitcaple. Fearing violence from Leslie, Crichton sought the services of the Marquis of Huntly's son, Viscount Aboyne, and the new laird of Rothiemay as part of an armed guard to protect him.

The men were lodged in the tower for the night. A terrible fire broke out and several people were killed – Viscount Aboyne, Gordon of Rothiemay, Colonel Ivat, English Will and their servants.

It was agreed that the fire had probably been started deliberately – Lady Crichton was the one upon whom most people's suspicions fell – but an official investigation that took place at Frendraught in 1631 was unsuccessful in finding enough evidence to blame any one individual, and the laird and his wife escaped any form of retribution.

The Lady of Frendraught apparently was troubled by her conscience after death, for she has returned to the scene of the crime several times since then. Her ghost, reportedly dressed in white, is traditionally never seen or heard by any laird of Frendraught, but other people, either living in the house or visiting it, have witnessed the presence of something supernatural, either seeing the figure of a lady or hearing loud sounds of raised voices and banging, which have no rational explanation.

Galdenoch Tower, Galloway

Galdenoch Tower dates from the sixteenth century. It was originally owned by nobility but after one hundred years or so it changed hands and became part of a farm.

The farmer's family at Galdenoch found themselves in the midst of the struggles of the Covenanters. The farmer was a staunch

Presbyterian and proud to have a son who took up the cause against the Royalists.

The Covenanter forces were losing the struggle, and the son found himself on the run, hounded by Royalist troops. Taking a chance that he would find an ally therein, he knocked at the door of an isolated farm one night and asked for shelter. The owner was initially hospitable, but after some time his attitude became more menacing. When the young Covenanter decided that it would be prudent to try to leave, his host attempted to prevent his departure by force. Terrified at the prospect of being handed over to the Royalist troops, the young man fought with his captor and killed him. He then fled for his life, back to Galdenoch. No one had seen him arriving or leaving the farmhouse, so he hoped that the dreadful secret of what he had done would never be discovered.

The young man's crime did go unpunished by law, but he had not seen the end of the man whom he had killed. At Galdenoch a few nights later, the young man was roused from sleep by the ghost of his victim. The ghost made further sleep impossible for the young man by throwing objects and furniture around the room, and laughing and shrieking maniacally. The ghost then set about tormenting the rest of the family, and soon all the inhabitants of the farm spent their days in dread and their nights in fear. For weeks on end the activities of the murdered man's spirit continued relentlessly. A minister was summoned to help, and he tried to exorcise the ghost, but the ghost was having none of it. The torment went on, night after night, week after week, until, driven to distraction, the family fled.

The ghost remained at Galdenoch, and when a new family moved in it started a campaign of mischief of another sort. For most of the time it was quiet, but then, unexpectedly, it would play sudden and dangerous tricks.

The family, sitting by the fire one night, were startled into frantic activity when a peat from the fire suddenly flew out of the hearth. Within moments, one of the outbuildings in the farm was ablaze.

On another occasion the malicious ghost lifted the grandmother of the family from her chair, carried her to a nearby stream, ducked her in the freezing water, lifted her out again and left her on a nearby wall, wet, shivering and frightened half to death.

Many attempts were made with the help of various members of the clergy to rid the tower of its unwanted inhabitant, but the ghost seemed to have the measure of anyone who came. It would taunt people with its demonic voice and laugh at their feeble attempts to banish it.

Finally, one particularly determined minister came to the house. Summoning a band of followers with good, strong voices, he took on the full force of the ghost. The minister and his helpers opened their psalm books and began to sing with gusto.

The ghost was stirred into activity by the sound of the singing and, rising to the challenge, began to sing its own songs in response, louder than the minister's choir. So the minister urged his people to sing louder as well. The louder the choir sang, the louder the ghost sang, until both parties were singing at top volume.

All night the minister urged his choir on as they worked their way through psalm after psalm. When all the psalms that they knew had been sung, they started with the first one again. The people in the choir were very tired and their voices were croaking, but still the minister urged them on, his voice rising above the others as he sought to outdo the ghost. As the first light of dawn glimmered in the distance, the ghost had to admit defeat. Finally, it had found a force stronger than it was. Its creaky voice was heard for the last time as it told the assembled crowd that it had given up.

The minister and his victorious forces, exhausted, made their way home. The ghost of Galdenoch was never seen again.

Inverawe House, Argyll

On the road west to Oban lies Taynuilt, where Inverawe House, owned by the family Campbell, keeps its own store of ghosts.

One room in the house is home to one of the many green ladies that frequent Scotland. Green Jean's origins are a matter for some debate, but one theory as to her identity has a particularly charming story attached to it.

Green Jean is believed to have been a woman called Mary Cameron, who lived in the seventeenth century. She was betrothed to Diarmid Campbell of Inverawe. Mary's family lived in a place called Callart House and, according to the legend that is told, Mary had upset her father, who had locked her in her room for a period as punishment. She must have been locked in the room for some time, for whilst she was confined, it is said, a Spanish ship carrying the plague arrived in Loch Leven, a small sea loch on the west coast. The infection spread rapidly, and before long all in the Cameron household had succumbed save Mary.

Left alone in the strangely quiet building, she was greatly relieved to hear sounds of activity outside. She called out to ask what was happening and was distressed to find that the noises outside were those of men who had been sent to burn the house down to clear away all traces of infection. When it was discovered that there was still someone alive in the house, a message was sent to Inverawe to ask for help. Diarmid Campbell arrived and released Mary, but they were unable to find shelter anywhere nearby, so frightened were the people of catching the plague. Not even Diarmid's family would offer them shelter. Diarmid and Mary were forced to struggle for survival out in the wild for quite some time before Campbell's father was convinced that neither carried the disease and allowed them to return to Inverawe, where they married and lived happily. The ghost of Mary Cameron returns to Inverawe, the place which must hold many happy memories for her.

The ghost of Duncan Campbell, resplendent in full Highland dress, is another that is said to haunt Inverawe.

In the early 1700s, Duncan's brother, Donald, was killed by Stewart of Appin in a fight. Having ended the life of Donald Campbell, Stewart then took himself to Inverawe House where Duncan, unaware as yet of his brother's death, offered hospitality.

The night after Stewart arrived, Duncan was tormented by the bloody figure of his brother appearing at his bedside, accusing him of making his murderer welcome, but he took no action. Finally, the ghostly figure gave up, but not before telling Duncan that he would meet him at Ticonderoga.

Duncan Campbell had no idea where Ticonderoga was until some years later, when serving with the Black Watch in America, he took part in an attack on a French fortress of the same name. He died from the injuries that he sustained in the battle – the ghost of his brother had finally been avenged.

At Inverawe House his figure returns from time to time, visiting the room that has been named after the battle where he lost his life.

Learmonth Gardens, Edinburgh

Learmonth Gardens is a quiet street in the respectable district of Comely Bank in the north of Edinburgh. One of the houses has a disturbing history. In the mid-1930s, the house was occupied by a baronet, Sir Alexander Seton, and his family. The family took a trip to Egypt and brought back a souvenir that they would later regret ever having set eyes upon.

The trip to Egypt incorporated a visit to the Temple of Luxor and in spite of the fact that it was illegal to remove anything from the tombs, Lady Seton picked up a small bone as a memento and brought it back to Scotland with her. The bone was placed in a glass case in the dining room.

The family had hardly settled back into normal life when strange and disturbing things started to happen. Crashing sounds were heard and furniture was found in disarray. Ornaments were found broken in rooms that had been empty. Lady Seton fell suddenly and inexplicably ill with a mystery complaint. Time and time again, the family was disturbed by strange occurrences for which no explanation could be found. Strangest of all was the sighting of a ghostly figure in long robes that appeared in the house to several people, residents and visitors alike. Servants of the family became unnerved and sought employment elsewhere.

At one point Sir Alexander lent the bone to a scientist friend.

Strangely, the ghostly figure disappeared from Learmonth Gardens for a while, only to be seen at the home of his friend. The family could no longer ignore the fact that the bone seemed to be responsible for the troubles that had been affecting them. Such a story could not remain a secret within the family for long, of course, and the Edinburgh newspapers were soon full of the news of the 'Curse of the Pharaoh', as they called it.

The bone was returned to Learmonth Gardens, and once more the furniture seemed to take on a life of its own. Sir Alexander himself became ill. Unable to withstand the strain any longer, Sir Alexander eventually surrendered the bone to a priest whom he knew. The bone was exorcised and then burnt. Thankfully, the torment came to an end when the bone was destroyed.

Leith Hall, Aberdeenshire

Leith Hall, Kennethmount, in Aberdeenshire is now a National Trust for Scotland property, but from its construction in the seventeenth century until 1945 it was owned by the Leith family. The family suffered a tragedy in 1763 when John Leith was shot by his wife, Elizabeth, during what is thought to have been a drunken argument. He died from his wounds. A ghost appeared to the people who were living in Leith Hall in the late 1960s which is thought to be that of the victim himself. Another ghost, a woman, is also believed to haunt the building. Her identity is not known.

An American writer called Elizabeth Byrd occupied part of the building with her husband, Barrie Gaunt. They both reported hearing strange noises for which they could find no obvious explanation and the sounds of footsteps and banging doors in parts of the house that they knew to be empty. Strange smells were noticed, too, similar to the scent of incense, and Byrd and her husband swore they could hear the sound of music playing and the drone of bagpipes. On one particular occasion, Barrie Gaunt saw the figure of a woman in one of the rooms they lived in. The figure was dressed in eighteenth-century clothing.

Elizabeth Byrd also reported that she found the atmosphere in the master bedroom most unsettling and that one night, as she slept in the large four-poster bed in that room, she awoke suddenly to see the figure of a man in Highland dress standing at the foot of the bed. The man's head was swathed in bandages, but from what she could see, he bore remarkable resemblance to the portrait of John Leith with which she was familiar.

Morningside, Edinburgh

Morningside is an area in the south of Edinburgh that has jokingly earned a nationwide reputation for being rather genteel and somewhat pretentious. Before Morningside grew into a suburb of the capital and acquired its 'fur coat and nae breeks' reputation, it was more of a rural area. Here, in 1712, a man called Sir Thomas Elphinstone purchased a large house when he retired from colonial life.

Sir Thomas was a widower – his wife had died when she gave birth to their only son, who was now grown up and had flown the nest. Sir Thomas's life in Morningside might have been destined to be rather a lonely one were it not for the fact that he was courting a young lady and hoping to marry her. The young lady's family was in favour of the match in spite of the considerable age difference between the two parties, but the young lady, Elizabeth Pittendale, was not quite so enamoured. Her heart belonged to another, an army officer called Jack Courage.

In spite of her misgivings, Elizabeth told Jack that they must end their relationship. Jack was about to be posted abroad, and the distance would help to sever the ties between the two of them. Elizabeth married Sir Thomas Elphinstone and settled in the house in Morningside.

It was a matter of months later that Sir Thomas told Elizabeth that she would be given the opportunity to meet his son, John, who was returning from military service abroad. When the young man arrived and was introduced to Elizabeth, however, she found it hard to behave as a stepmother might, for Sir Thomas's son, John, was none other than the young man she had known and loved as Jack Courage.

It was inevitable that their relationship would resume and, accordingly, that it would be discovered by Sir Thomas. They could not keep their feelings for each other a secret for long. Sir Thomas entered a room one day to find his son and his wife engaged in a passionate embrace. Filled with rage, Sir Thomas attacked his son, who fought back with all his strength. Elizabeth, distraught to see such violence, tried to intervene and was stabbed accidentally by Sir Thomas. The wound was fatal. When Sir Thomas realised what had happened, he was heartbroken. He killed himself. Husband and wife were buried together in the family vault.

John survived but left the house, renting it out to an acquaintance. The new tenant was the first to see the ghostly figure of a weeping lady walking down the corridor to one of the bedrooms. The man was not frightened by the ghost but was sad to see her in such distress. He sought the help of a medium, who told him that Elizabeth's spirit could not be at peace as long as she was buried beside her killer.

John was informed of this and at once arranged for Elizabeth's body to be moved. The ghost was never again seen in the house in Morningside. When John himself died a few years later, he was buried, according to his wishes, beside his sweetheart, Elizabeth.

New Lanark, Lanarkshire

New Lanark is a historic village at the edge of the market town of Lanark. It was built in the 1780s by the Glasgow banker and cotton merchant David Dale as a social experiment. Workers in the mills in New Lanark had better working conditions than many of their contemporaries elsewhere, and there was also provision for the education and welfare of their families. The village is now a World Heritage site.

It took thirty years for two people from New Lanark to find out that they had both had the experience of seeing the same ghost when they were children. The two were Mary Graham and her brother Alan who, when they were young, had lived with their parents in a flat above the family shop in New Lanark just after the turn of the nineteenth century.

The first to see the ghost had been Alan. The other members of the family had gone out for a while to visit his grandmother, leaving him alone in the house in bed. He had woken up feeling strangely cold and had seen the figure of a woman at his window. The woman was dressed in Highland clothes and she was knitting. She had walked towards the child and then passed him by, walking right through the closed bedroom door.

Alan had been very frightened by the experience, but his parents had told him quite firmly that it was nothing more than a dream, so no more was said about it.

Some time later, his sister Mary saw an identical figure in the flat. She was older than Alan. When she told her parents about what she had experienced, they admitted that what she had seen was probably a ghost. Mary was instructed that she was not to tell her brother, for he would be frightened and would not sleep at night. Mary's parents believed that the ghost meant no harm and probably had some connection with the shop below the flat, which had been at one time a doctor's surgery. Perhaps the woman had died as a result of, or in spite of, medical treatment she had received there. Perhaps she was the victim of something altogether more suspicious – no one could tell.

The tartan cape that the woman wore was possibly a clue as to where she came from originally. Many of the mill workers in New Lanark had come from the Highlands. Perhaps the ghost had been among those who had come to New Lanark to work.

Mary Graham did as her parents had told her – she never said a word to her brother Alan. It was only when they had both grown up that Alan spoke to her of his own encounter with the mystery woman. Finally, brother and sister discovered that they had both seen the same ghost.

Queensberry House, Edinburgh

Queensberry House, in Edinburgh's Canongate, was used in its last years as a hospital for the long-term care of the elderly and infirm. It is now demolished.

It was first built in the 1680s as a home for William Douglas, the first Duke of Queensberry. The Duke spent a great deal of time at Queensberry House, preferring life in the capital to staying at Drumlanrig Castle, his other residence.

A disturbing story about Queensberry House gave rise to reports that it was haunted.

It is said that there was one particular member of Queensberry's family who was insane. He was a powerful man and had to spend most of his life in confinement within the family home, both for his own safety and that of others.

One night, however, he was left at Queensberry House, locked in his room while the rest of the household went visiting elsewhere overnight. Only a kitchen hand remained at Queensberry House, tending to the kitchen fire.

The young lad was dozing by the fire when he was disturbed by the sound of footsteps. Rousing himself and sitting up, he was horrified to see the madman standing in the doorway of the kitchen. He had broken out of his room. The poor lad froze in terror as the madman came towards him, a maniacal gleam in his eye. The kitchen hand was young, small and slight. He was no match for his powerful opponent. Nor could he reason with his attacker – how can you reason with someone who has no grasp of reality whatsoever? He was helpless, abandoned to his fate at the hands of a lunatic.

The fate of the kitchen hand was dreadful. Terrible visions of his torment were to fill the nights of the rest of the household with terrible dreams for a long time to come. When they returned the next day to Queensberry House, the kitchen fire had gone out but the terrible smell of burning flesh filled the air. In the kitchen, they found the charred remains of the boy still tied to the spit where he had spent his last agonising moments. He had, quite literally, been roasted alive.

The cries of the kitchen hand were to be heard in the old kitchen at Queensberry House for many years afterwards.

Other Haunted Houses

Compared to most of the buildings that have found their way into this book, one particular house in Edinburgh, being much less than a century old, is a surprisingly 'young' place to find itself haunted. The house is in Stevenson Drive, on the western side of the city. The occupant, newly widowed, was stunned to see writing appearing on one of the inside walls. The man thought that perhaps his dead wife was trying to contact him from the afterlife, but as the scribblings on the wall were indecipherable, it was impossible to work out what she was trying to say, if indeed it was her work. After a short period, the writing stopped as mysteriously as it had begun, and no one was any the wiser as to who, or what, might have caused the phenomenon.

Another house in Edinburgh, in Hazeldean Terrace in the Liberton area, was the scene of vigorous activity by some sort of ghostly presence for a period of time. The activities, similar to those of a poltergeist, stopped quite suddenly after a period of three years or so.

Quite a few ghosts are said to inhabit houses in the granite city of Aberdeen in the northeast of Scotland. The shadowy figure of a young woman is said to haunt one particular house – the ghost of a young servant who was unjustly accused of theft by her employers. Driven to despair at having to live with the shame of their accusations, the young girl felt compelled to take her own life.

Another house is said to have been the 'home' of quite a friendly ghost. The figure was that of a man, wearing a large hat and a cloak. Children in the family were well used to seeing him and were not afraid, but apparently when their mother caught sight of the phantom one day, she spoke to him firmly and advised him to leave as she did not want the children to be disturbed. The ghost, it would seem, took heed of her words and moved off elsewhere, for the family did not see him again. Who he was, and why he appeared, was never known.

A cottage in Fife is said to be one place where at least three ghosts share the accommodation quite harmoniously with its living occupants. It seems that when a young couple first moved into the cottage and began working on it to modernise it to their own tastes, strange poltergeist-type activities began to bother them. After a time, it would appear that ghosts and mortals have become accustomed to each other's ways, and the living occupants find it quite comforting to come home to a place that has signs of life in it, rather than a dark empty house with no one at home.

HOTELS AND PUBLIC HOUSES: EXTRA GUESTS

The Scots have a reputation for their hospitality, but guests in some of the country's hotels and pubs, both old and new, might just find that they get a little more than they have paid for. Landladies who refuse to leave their territory even after death, spectres of former guests with mysterious histories, anonymous presences that tease and torment the unsuspecting visitor – these are just some of the ghosts that haunt various establishments countrywide. The following stories are just a selection of the numerous strange tales that the pubs and hotels of Scotland have to tell. The older inns in particular make many a visitor's stay all the more worthwhile when the presence of something supernatural makes itself apparent. Should you find yourself stopping for a drink or a meal in an old Scottish pub or inn, you would be well advised to inquire within whether there are any extra, non-paying guests in the place. In some places it will take several strong drinks before you can start to see things, but in others you can have the strangest experiences even if you are completely teetotal.

Port Ellen, Islay

The island of Islay, off the west coast of Scotland, is of interest both to nature lovers and whisky lovers. It is a bird-watcher's paradise and also, on account of its distilleries, a haven for the connoisseur of fine malt whisky.

One former distillery on the island, close to the town of Port Ellen, was converted many years ago for use as a hotel. The hotel is said to be haunted by the ghost of a man. Visitors to the hotel have seen the figure of a thickset man in one of the corridors. One visitor in particular claimed to have been troubled by a recurrent dream of falling from a great height while staying at the hotel.

The story that is told to explain these occurrences would be amusing were it not for the fact that it has such a tragic ending. Apparently, when the building was still in use as a distillery in the nineteenth century, an enterprising and thirsty rogue with a taste for a good drop of malt broke in one night. He must have had a lovely time once he had found his way in. He climbed to the second floor, found himself with a good quantity of whisky and settled down to enjoy himself. Obviously, he drank more than a drop – who wouldn't, after all, if given the chance to imbibe as freely as this?

After some time the burglar must have decided that enough was enough and he ought to be getting back home to his bed. A pleasant fog had settled around his brain by this time, however, and he was not entirely sure how to find his way out of the building. Which way had he come in? Unconcerned, he decided that he could not be bothered trying to retrace his steps and, instead, attempted to make his escape through the nearest window. Our hapless hero had forgotten, however, that he was on the second floor of the distillery. The nearest window was a long way from the ground, and he was killed by the impact of the fall.

The window from which the unfortunate burglar jumped was sealed up during the conversion work on the building, but his ghost still appears in the hotel from time to time, around the place where he met his death.

The Cross Keys Hotel, Peebles

> Ye came, ye went,
> But I hiv steyed
> Fit three hunder years

Several ghosts have been seen in various places in and around the pretty town of Peebles on the River Tweed. The Cross Keys Hotel in particular has quite a reputation for having an extra guest. Perhaps 'extra guest' is not such an appropriate term to use, for the ghost is that of Marion Ritchie, who was once the landlady of the inn. On hearing about the things that she gets up to, it is tempting to wonder whether Miss Ritchie resents the fact that the establishment over which she once presided is now in the hands of others. Perhaps she dislikes the modern world. Whatever motivates her ghost, she likes to cause trouble, although, so far, the trouble has not been serious. Things are moved from place to place, and crockery and glasses are broken. She makes her presence felt from time to time in various parts of the hotel, and people claim even to have heard her voice. Miss Ritchie's speciality is tampering with electrical goods, switching things on and off to cause irritation and consternation. Is this a sign of the good woman's contempt for all things modern or is she merely fascinated with the wonders of technology?

In 1975 the hotel attracted the interest of a group of investigators who brought recording equipment into the hotel to try to capture Miss Ritchie's voice on tape. They set up their machines and settled in to wait for some action. Obligingly, Miss Ritchie made herself heard. The investigators were delighted. They had captured the voice of a ghost on tape! However, the playback was distorted and useless. They tried again but were rewarded with a soundless tape. Much the same thing happened with a third attempt, in spite of the fact that before setting up for recording, all equipment was checked meticulously and sound levels carefully set. It seemed that they had been the victims of another of Miss Ritchie's little tricks.

The Clydesdale Hotel, Lanark

Lanark is a busy market town in the south of central Scotland. The Clydesdale Hotel is an old building in the town, built around the end of the eighteenth century.

Long before the hotel was built, the site had been occupied by a Franciscan priory at some time in the fourteenth century. In the cellars of the hotel, staff have often reported feeling strange sensations, like sensing a figure passing silently by in the darkness, and hearing strange noises unrelated to the sounds of the hotel above them. The figure of a monk is also reputed to have been seen down there.

The Covenanter Hotel, Falkland

In the picturesque and historic royal burgh of Falkland in Fife stands the Covenanter Hotel, a building some three or more centuries old but internally altered considerably over the years. The hotel is the haunt of a female figure who has been seen floating around the bedrooms from time to time. No one can be certain of the identity of the woman. Some have claimed that it is the unhappy spirit of Mary Queen of Scots, who lived for a while at nearby Falkland Palace. The ghost of Mary Queen of Scots, however, is also said to haunt several other places in Scotland. Like the ghost of Bonnie Prince Charlie, Mary's spirit is one that more sites would like to lay claim to than are credible.

The Kylesku Inn, Sutherland

The Kylesku Inn is in Sutherland in the northwest of Scotland. It is situated by the bridge of the same name, just beside the old ferry berth. The story that is told in connection with the ghost that haunts the hotel has a touch of Whisky Galore about it. This story, however, does not end happily.

A ship was wrecked in the waters off the Minch sometime in the eighteenth century, and some of the cargo from the wreckage was eventually washed ashore. One lucky fisherman discovered a barrel of whisky that had survived a battering by the waves. Very pleased with his find, he heaved it up to the ferry house at Kylesku (now the Inn) and dragged it up to the loft to hide it.

The fisherman threw a little party that Saturday night, inviting a few of his friends up to the loft to share in his good fortune. Time passed and the gathering grew rather riotous. No one seemed to care that it was nearly midnight and the Sabbath was drawing near.

At this point, versions of the story differ. One version claims that it was the fisherman who tried to calm things down and bring an end to the celebrations, while another tells us that the fisherman's son was the one who became alarmed at the way things were turning out and tried to get his father to stop the party.

Whatever happened in fact will probably never be known for sure, but there was a struggle between the fisherman and his son. The fisherman was thrown down the ladder from the loft. His neck was broken, and he died. Before he breathed his last, however, he was heard to utter a dreadful curse upon his son. He would return to get his revenge. It is said that the fisherman's son was killed at sea not many months afterwards.

The fisherman himself, in spite of having got his revenge, still returns to the inn once in a while, appearing near the place where he fell to his death. Perhaps he is looking for one last sip of that whisky he found.

The Learmonth Hotel, Edinburgh

The Learmonth Hotel is conveniently situated for tourists in the capital city, for it is close to the west end of Princes' Street, the beautiful main route through the centre of town. It is part of a stately terrace that was built in the nineteenth century. Visitors to the Learmonth Hotel are often fascinated as much by the ghost that haunts the building as they are by the many attractions that Edinburgh has to offer.

It is quite a mischievous presence, by all accounts, but seems to be harmless in spite of the bother it causes. It has a cheerful disposition, apparently, for staff and visitors to the hotel have heard the sound of its ghostly whistling in the corridors.

The spirit plays pranks on guests from time to time, on occasion locking them out of their rooms. At other times doors are found to have opened or closed themselves and doors that had been locked have been found unlocked.

The ghost in the Learmonth Hotel has other party tricks in

addition to all this – tricks that are very similar to those that Marion Ritchie, the ghost of the Cross Keys Hotel in Peebles (see page 127) likes to play. It plays with electrical apparatus, irritating staff and guests when it switches kettles and hairdryers on and off.

The ghost's identity is not known, but its presence makes a stay at the Learmonth Hotel even more interesting.

The Moncrieffe Arms, Bridge of Earn

The Moncrieffe Arms is in Bridge of Earn, Perthshire, a few miles from the town of Perth. Many visitors to the hotel have had stories to tell of strange noises in the guest rooms. The landlord has also been witness to some curious goings-on, including something unseen apparently taking the opportunity to have a bath while the rest of the guests were out.

The landlord was walking along the corridor past the bathroom one day when he noticed that the door was closed. Through the door he could hear the sounds of someone taking a bath. The landlord was a little puzzled, for he thought that all the hotel guests were out, but he was not concerned. Perhaps he had been mistaken and someone was still there.

Moments later, however, coming back past the bathroom, the landlord found the bathroom door was open again. When he looked in through the door, he could see no sign of anyone having had a bath recently. There were no drips on the floor, no steamy atmosphere, no wet towels . . .

The mystery deepened when the landlord found out later that, as he had initially thought, none of the guests had been in the hotel at the time.

The Old Post Horn Inn, Crawford

The Old Post Horn Inn in Crawford, Lanarkshire, was originally a coaching inn on the road from south to north. The original building dates from 1744. It would come as no surprise to find that the inn was haunted by the ghosts of fallen Jacobite men, for the trees in the woods nearby were used to hang a few supporters of the Jacobite cause in the rebellion of 1745. However, the inn is not known for being haunted by any such ghosts. The ghost at the Old Post Horn is instead that of a little girl, who is heard singing and playing in the area of the dining room. She is thought to have been the young daughter of a one-time landlord of the inn. The dining room stands on the site of the old stables, and it is said that the little girl was especially fond of horses and spent a great deal of time there. She was playing outside when she died, tragically killed by a coach and horses visiting her father's establishment.

Pannanich Wells Hotel, Ballater

Ballater is a beautiful town in Deeside, a spa town frequented in Victorian times by the rich and influential, who sought benefit to their health from taking the waters there. The Pannanich Wells Hotel in the town dates from the middle of the eighteenth century and was most favourably mentioned by Her Royal Majesty Queen Victoria in the journal that she kept.

As well as having the honour of being visited by Queen Victoria, the Pannanich Wells Hotel has another claim to fame. It is the haunt of a grey lady, the ghost of an elegant young woman dressed in a grey blouse and a long grey skirt. The Grey Lady has been seen by various people both in and around the building. Sometimes the ghost cannot be seen, but instead people have heard noises such as doors opening and closing without apparent reason. The Grey Lady is not a ghost that causes great alarm, and indeed she is regarded with a certain amount of affection by those who are familiar with the hotel.

Tibbie Shiel's Inn, Peebles

In the early 1820s a young woman from the Borders by the name of Isabella Shiel found herself widowed. She was an enterprising person, and in order to feed herself and pay the rent, she opened her cottage to passing travellers, offering food and drink and letting out one of the rooms. The cottage, situated between Moffat and Selkirk, soon became a very popular stopping-off point, for Tibbie Shiel's hospitality and cooking were fine indeed. Her visitors were not only travellers. Many famous literary figures of the time and scholars and religious men took to gathering at the inn, taking advantage of the chance to meet in convivial surroundings and to enjoy good food, fine ale and stimulating conversation. Amongst the well-known visitors to the inn were James Hogg ('the Ettrick Shepherd'), Robert Louis Stevenson and Sir Walter Scott.

Tibbie Shiel died in 1878, but the original inn, greatly extended over the years, still exists. The inn holds on to the ghost of its original landlady with a certain amount of pride, and visitors have claimed that Tibbie's presence can still be felt as she pushes through the crowd of customers on her way to warm herself at her favourite spot by the fire.

The White Dove Hotel, Aberdeen

The White Dove Hotel in Aberdeen has been demolished, but the story of its haunting is well known.

One of the guests at the hotel had fallen sick. The woman was an actress, apparently, and her name was Miss Vining. She had become quite ill shortly after her arrival at the hotel. When a doctor was called to examine her, he decided that she was suffering from a rare disease, thought to be tropical in origin. The patient's condition grew worse and was causing concern. The doctor pronounced that she required constant care, so a nurse was called in to attend to her.

The nurse noticed a strange, eerie atmosphere in the room when she arrived, but put it down to the condition of her patient and the stormy weather raging outside. Miss Vining was too ill to speak, so the nurse spent some time attending to practicalities, monitoring her patient's condition and assuring her comfort, and then settled in a chair beside the bed to wait quietly beside her, reading.

After a while something made the nurse look up. Her eyes passed over her sleeping patient and came to rest on another chair at the opposite side of the bed. There, seated quietly, was the figure of a small girl. It was hard to make out the child's features, for she was wearing a large hat. The first reaction of the nurse was to protest with the child: how and why had she come into the sickroom without permission? But as the nurse rose from her seat, the child raised a hand to motion her back. The child seemed to be possessed of some strange power, for the nurse found that she could not move any farther. The nurse then tried to turn to her patient, who was showing some signs of distress. Once again, she found she was unable to move. It was the oddest feeling. She sat back in her chair, and although she had not been feeling tired at all, she could not prevent herself from falling asleep.

When the nurse woke up, the child had gone, but Miss Vining was delirious with a raging fever and needed attention. The nurse, thankfully, was now able to rise and care for her. When morning came, the nurse told the doctor about the child who had been in the room. He gave strict instructions that Miss Vining was too ill to be visited by anyone. The following night, he said, the nurse was to lock the door behind her when she took up her post by her patient's bedside.

The nurse did as she was told. The next night she made absolutely sure that she was alone in the room with Miss Vining. Then she locked the door firmly behind her, ready to start her shift.

Miss Vining was comfortable and peaceful, so the nurse sat by her bed for a while. She nodded off for a few moments, and when she stirred she saw the little girl in the room, just as before. Once again, when she tried to shoo the child away, the little girl raised her hand and the nurse was unable to do a thing. She was virtually paralysed.

Miss Vining's condition grew markedly worse, and the nurse was distressed to see this, but the child still held her under some sort of spell. There was nothing she could do to help her patient. At length, after what seemed to be an interminable time, watching helplessly as Miss Vining tossed and moaned in her delirium, the nurse saw the child rise from her seat and make for the window.

Finding that she was free to move, the nurse made a grab for the little girl, knocking her hat from her head. To her horror, she saw that the girl's face was that of a corpse. She was an Indian child and had obviously been very beautiful, but it was clear that her throat had been cut and now her face was twisted in death. The nurse fainted.

When the nurse came round, the child had gone and Miss Vining was dead.

Afterwards, when hotel staff were packing up the belongings of the deceased, it is said that they found a photograph of a child, which the nurse identified as being the same child she had seen in ghostly form. On the back of the photograph were written these words:

Natalie. May God forgive us.

Nobody could find out any more, for after the death of Miss Vining, the little girl was never seen again.

MILITARY SPECTRES

Over the centuries, the Highlands and Lowlands of Scotland have seen many a bloody battle as rival clans raged one against the other, or as Scots united against their enemies, particularly the English. It can be hard to imagine the horror of the hand-to-hand fighting of days gone by. The suffering that those many thousands who were wounded had to endure as they lay bleeding on the battlefields must have been immense. The bravery of the Scottish soldier in battle is legendary – the Scots were a nation of proud fighting men. Nevertheless, it was without doubt a test of even the bravest men's courage to have to fight for clan or country. The brutal consequences of some of these terrible struggles of ancient times can still be felt most acutely by those who are witness to the ghostly presences that hover near some of the old battlegrounds, even to this day.

Culloden, Inverness

Culloden was the battle that sounded the death knell for the Jacobite forces. Here, in 1746, they were defeated. Hopes for the return of a Stewart to the throne of Scotland were dashed once and for all. Bonnie Prince Charlie escaped from the battle by a stroke of good fortune and fled overseas. His followers were not so fortunate. The Jacobite forces had arrived at Culloden in poor condition. After a fruitless journey down south in an attempt to muster support, they had returned to Scotland diminished in numbers and exhausted after many days of marching in atrocious conditions. They were vastly overwhelmed, both in numbers and strength, by 'Butcher' Cumberland's men. The battle was a slaughter.

The spectres of those who lost their lives are still in evidence on the field of Culloden, especially on the anniversary of the battle, 16 April. Marching Highlanders, bleeding men, corpses – all are said to have been seen. Noises of battle, such as clashing swords, gunfire and the cries of the wounded, are reported from time to time. One ghostly figure that has appeared is that of a tall young man dressed as a Highlander, thoroughly dejected and despairing. He has been heard to murmur what sounds to be the word 'defeated'.

Close to the battle site is Culloden House where Bonnie Prince Charlie reputedly slept the night before the battle. The house, which is now a hotel, still has the bed where he is supposed to have slept and a stick that is said to have belonged to him. Culloden House is one of the places where the ghost of the prince is said to have been seen, resplendent in full Highland dress.

Glencoe, Argyll

Glencoe is not so much a battle site as the scene of a slaughter. The Massacre of Glencoe is one of the most infamous events in Scottish history. In February 1692, a company of soldiers of the clan Campbell took horrible and brutal action against the clan Mac-Donald. They did this in the most cowardly manner, accepting the hospitality of the MacDonalds, then surprising them by night and slaughtering many of them as they slept. Forty or so MacDonalds lost their lives.

Glencoe is a popular haunt for climbers, who come to challenge themselves on the surrounding mountainsides. On a fine day, the glen is spectacular to behold, a place of outstanding beauty and grandeur, but the weather, fickle and dangerous as it is in these parts, can change in moments. Then the hills and the glen can take on another profile, just as impressive but awesomely so.

The MacDonalds still haunt the glen. Various people have seen ghostly appearances that bear witness to the dreadful atrocity that was committed against them all those years ago. The anniversary of the massacre, 13 February, is the time at which the phantoms are most likely to appear. The weather is at its bleakest at this time of year and the air can turn even chillier at the sight of the still, staring figures of the MacDonalds. It will turn coldest of all for those who go by the name of Campbell.

The Hill of the Battle, Highlands

A story is told by a Scots writer of his own ghostly experiences near his home in a remote part of the Highlands.

The writer's house was in a particularly isolated spot, above a deep wooded gully through which flowed a small but rapid river. On the other side of the river was a high ridge, with small hills at its northern end. The writer had lived in the house for some time and had often been puzzled to hear what sounded like bagpipes playing in the distance. He was accustomed to the sound of the pipes and recognised the noise that he heard as being the sound of a lone piper playing two-drone pipes – the kind of pipes that had been played in Scotland some two or three centuries before. Modern pipes have a third drone and sound quite different.

The writer marvelled at how the sound of playing could travel such a distance – his house was some two miles or so from any other habitation. As he continued hearing the sound from time to time, always coming from the same direction, he took it upon himself to make some enquiries in the district to find out who the piper was. He was surprised to learn that there was no one living in the surrounding area who played the pipes. His curiosity was further aroused when he heard that the man who had lived in his house before him had also spoken of hearing the sounds of piping. Where was the sound coming from?

The writer tried to think of some logical explanation for the sounds that he was hearing. Could it be the noise of the water below his house? Or the sound of the wind in the trees? Sometimes, when he heard the pipes, he would take himself outside and walk in the direction from which the sound was coming. He would listen to the wind and the water. He travelled quite some distance, listening carefully all the time, but nothing could convince him that the noises he was hearing were made by anything other than bagpipes. It seemed that there was no explanation for the phenomenon, and the writer had no choice but to give up his investigations and simply enjoy the music whenever he was given the opportunity.

This he did, until one night early in the following year when he had gone to bed late and just dropped off to sleep. He had been for a walk earlier, enjoying the clear skies and the fresh air, and he had heard the pipes playing. But, of course, this was not unusual. He had not been long asleep when he woke to hear a tremendous racket coming from outside. It sounded, indeed, like the noise of ferocious fighting. Men's voices roared and screamed through the night air, punctuated by the sounds of clashing swords. The lone piper could not be heard this time. Instead, the writer heard the sound of several sets of pipes, rising above the sounds of battle.

The clamour outside was very frightening, but in spite of this, the writer felt obliged to investigate. Flinging on some clothes over his night attire, he descended the stairs towards the front door with a great deal of trepidation. As he reached the door, he realised that he could no longer hear the noise of fighting. The 'battle', if that was what it was, appeared to have come to an end, but he could still hear a great deal of activity going on – clattering and clanking, and the sounds of marching feet. The noise seemed to be coming from the direction of the hills at the end of the ridge, and it was getting louder all the time. He could make out the sounds of people crossing the river below the house and coming nearer. He could hear voices too – men's voices calling out in victory, or so it seemed. And still the pipes played, triumphantly.

The writer went outside and let his three dogs out of the byre. They ran towards the sounds, barking furiously, but within moments the eldest dog was back, whining and cowed. The other two dogs, who were no more than puppies, seemed to take fright and sped off, yelping, across the hillside and out of sight.

The army, by the sound of it, was still getting nearer and nearer, but the writer could see not a soul. To the eyes, the entire area all around was deserted; to the ears, on the other hand, it was teeming with warriors.

The writer stood rooted to the spot as the unseen army passed noisily right by him; pipers, soldiers – even women's voices were audible amidst the cacophony. Although it seemed as if he was right in the middle of the throng, nothing and no one touched him. The phantom army seemed to pass straight through the writer's home, oblivious of the stout stone walls that stood in its way. Gradually the sounds began to fade as the ghostly troops marched on into the distance.

The writer experienced the strange episode only once. After that, he still heard the sound of the lone piper at regular intervals while he lived in the house, but the phantom army never returned. It could have come only from a time long past. The writer tells that the hill from which the sounds of fighting came that night is called in Gaelic Mam a' Chatha, the Hill of the Battle.

Killiecrankie, Perthshire

The Battle of Killiecrankie took place in 1689 between the Jaco-bites and the forces of William III under the leadership of General Hugh Mackay. The site of the battle is nearly three miles northwest of Pitlochry, in Perthshire. The Jacobites were victorious, but their leader, Viscount John Graham of Claverhouse, known as Bonnie Dundee, was killed in the fray. In spite of the victorious outcome of the battle for the Jacobite forces, the death of Dundee was a tragic blow to their cause.

Nowadays there is a visitor centre at the battle site, which is in the care of the National Trust for Scotland, and Killiecrankie is a popular venue for school parties on history trips and for tourists from all over the world.

Different experiences are associated with the battle site. Some people have reported seeing an eerie red glow. Some claim to have seen groups of soldiers marching as if into battle. Others have re-ported seeing a ghostly version of the battle itself, or at least a part of it. One particular story tells of a woman seeing the bodies of sev-eral dead English officers around her feet as she picnicked at Killie-crankie. Most of these stories come from people who have been visiting the site around the time of the anniversary of the battle, which is 27 July.

Two more stories connected with the Battle of Killiecrankie and the death of Bonnie Dundee are told in another chapter in this book, 'Prophecies, Signs and Curses' (page 163).

Montrose Airfield

It is not the sound of pipes and clashing swords or the sight of Highland warriors that have earned the old airfield at Montrose a reputation as a haunted place. The several ghosts at Montrose come from an era when battle had become considerably more mechanised.

Montrose airfield was built as a base for the Royal Flying Corps (later to become the Royal Air Force) not long before the First World War. The first ghost associated with the airfield, now the site of a museum, dates from its early days in 1913, when a biplane, piloted by Lieutenant Desmond Arthur of No. 2 Squadron, Royal Flying Corps, came apart in mid-air and crashed to the ground in a field not far from the aerodrome. The ghostly figure of an airman, thought to be Desmond Arthur, has been seen several times since then. There have also been reports of a phantom biplane, seen in the skies around the airfield by other pilots in the years following the tragedy. On one occasion the ghost plane was nearly the cause of another crash. Another time a pilot witnessed the ghostly re-enactment of the terrible disaster in 1913.

In addition to the ghosts of Desmond Arthur and his biplane, there have been sightings of another ghostly airman and also of a phantom Second World War bomber in the skies above Montrose.

Nechtanesmere, Angus

The ghosts of Nechtanesmere date from very early Scottish history. The Battle of Nechtanesmere, by Dunnichen Hill in Angus, was fought in the late seventh century AD between the Northumbrians and the Picts. The Picts, led by Brude mac Bile, were victorious over the Northumbrian men of King Ecgfrith. The battle put an end to the Northumbrians' progress northwards. King Ecgfrith and most of his men were killed.

One report of haunting close to the site of the Battle of Nechtanesmere dates from 1950, when a middle-aged woman called Miss E. F. Smith had a strange experience while driving home from Brechin to Letham one night. It was January, and snow had fallen. Miss Smith's car skidded on the newly fallen snow and went off the road into a ditch. Unable to get her car back on the road without assistance, Miss Smith had no alternative but to walk the remaining seven or eight miles of her journey.

She was nearly at Letham when she caught sight of flaming torchlight in the distance. As she drew near to Dunnichen Hill, she saw men in ancient garb – brown tunics and leggings – wandering around in a field nearby. They kept their eyes to the ground, where the bodies of other men lay. The figures were oblivious of Miss Smith as they moved silently around.

It would appear that Miss Smith was witness to the ghostly figures of survivors of the Battle of Nechtanesmere searching the battlefield for their dead and dying comrades.

DRAMATIC APPEARANCES

People in the theatrical professions have a reputation for being superstitious. Many actors and actresses will freely admit to owning one or more lucky charms and following their own personal little rituals, which they believe will bring them luck during their performances. In addition to personal lucky charms and rituals, there are also theatrical superstitions that are quite well known to the public in general. For example, one should never wish performers 'good luck' before they go on stage, for this is believed to have the opposite of the desired effect. Instead, a hearty 'break a leg!' is thought to be a safer means of wishing a performer success.

Shakespeare's *Macbeth* has its own superstitious associations. Members of the acting profession believe that it is unlucky to call the play by name. It is referred to instead as 'The Scottish Play'.

In such circles, where people come together who are both collectively and individually superstitious and who are required by their profession to be imaginative and intuitive, it will hardly come as a surprise to those of a more sceptical nature that many theatres throughout Great Britain, and in Scotland in particular, are said to be haunted. Nonetheless, witnesses to the presence of some of these ghosts do not necessarily belong to the theatrical professions, and it is not easy to find alternative explanations for all the ghosts that are said to exist.

The Byre Theatre, St Andrews

The Byre Theatre, converted in the 1930s from a dairy, is a small but thriving establishment in the historic university town of St Andrews in Fife. Throughout the year a succession of performances are put on for audiences of all ages. The scope of productions ranges from serious works to pantomime, and most are well attended. In spite of the difficulties of the time, the theatre was kept going right through the dark years of the Second World War thanks to the unstinting efforts of its director, Charles Manford.

It would appear that Charles Manford's dedication to the Byre has stayed with him after death. He seems to be reluctant to leave his beloved theatre entirely in the hands of others, for although he died in 1955 his ghost still haunts backstage at the Byre. It makes its presence felt with a district chill in the air. The ghost does no harm – perhaps because the theatre still flourishes.

His Majesty's Theatre, Aberdeen

His Majesty's Theatre was built in 1904 and has been the venue for a great variety of performances since then. In the early 1940s the theatre saw tragedy when one of the stagehands working there, a man called Jake, was killed in an accident by a stage hoist.

Jake still haunts the theatre, and a variety of strange happenings, from disappearing objects to shadowy appearances and strange noises, are associated with his ghost.

The Theatre Royal, Edinburgh

The Theatre Royal was built in 1768 on the site that is now occupied by the General Post Office, at the corner of Waterloo Place and the North Bridge in Edinburgh. The theatre was in operation for less than one hundred years – it closed down in 1859 – and yet even in that relatively short period it acquired a reputation for being haunted.

The stage manager of the theatre lived with his family in a flat at the top of the building, above the auditorium, and they were the first to notice strange goings-on. At night, when the theatre was empty and everything was locked up, the sounds of voices, footsteps and general activity could be heard from inside. It appeared that ghostly players were returning to the theatre for spooky, nocturnal performances of their own.

The ghosts of the Theatre Royal became quite famous around

Edinburgh, but when the theatre was pulled down in 1859 to make way for the new Post Office building, the ghosts seemed to vanish – perhaps to make an entrance elsewhere.

Edinburgh – Three More Ghostly Theatres

The Royal Lyceum, still a popular venue for theatregoers in the capital, The Playhouse, which is now used as a venue for rock concerts and musicals, and the Edinburgh Festival Theatre, rescued from existence as a bingo hall and restored to theatrical glory, are all said to be haunted.

The Playhouse

The ghost in The Playhouse is known affectionately as Albert, and although nobody is certain as to who he might have been his presence manifests itself in a variety of ways. He is a mischievous ghost who plays tricks, apparently. People have felt his presence in certain 'cold spots' in the theatre. He has been seen, on occasion, as a figure in a grey coat.

The Royal Lyceum

The Royal Lyceum is believed to be haunted by a woman. She has been seen by performers on stage, who have spotted her figure high up in a gallery of the theatre now used only for lighting.

Edinburgh Festival Theatre

Staff at the Festival Theatre claim to have seen the tall, dark, shadowy figure of a man on a number of occasions. There is speculation that this might be the ghost of the Great Lafayette, a magician who was killed in a fire at the theatre in the days when it was known as The Empire.

The Theatre Royal, Glasgow

The Theatre Royal in Glasgow is home nowadays to Scottish Opera, but apparently it has another resident performer who puts in an appearance from time to time. She is known as Nora, reputedly a woman who worked as a cleaner in the theatre some years ago. Some say that she desperately wanted to be an actress and sought employment in the theatre, hoping that she would then get the chance to act. She eventually secured herself an audition with a director at the theatre but was virtually laughed off the stage. Heart-broken, she committed suicide.

MIND HOW YOU GO

Numerous and varied are the ghosts that are said to haunt Scotland's thoroughfares. It might be a city street or a country road, a dark corner in a dingy district or a sunlit path through a panoramic glen. Fields, mountains and waterways all have their spectral presences. There are ghosts on land and sea, in places of solitude and by bustling visitor centres. Ghosts appear wherever people have been and wherever they might go. Many ghosts haunt particular buildings or ruins, but others frequent areas that are not bound by walls. Mention has been made of some of these ghosts already – Major Weir, who strides out and rides in his carriage in the area of the West Bow in Edinburgh; Angus Roy, with his damaged leg scraping behind him along Victoria Terrace; the soldiers marching through the Pass of Killiecrankie. Some of the ghosts are nameless, while the identities of others are well known. But the tales of these ghosts just might make the reader stop and think wherever they go – who was here before me? What happened? Who might be watching?

Annan

The bizarre occurrences on the A75 near Annan were comparatively recent compared to many other tales of ghostly apparitions around Scotland. They took place in the 1960s. The fact that two young men were simultaneous witnesses to all that happened gives credence to the tale. Had there been only one of them to tell what happened, it is unlikely that he would have been believed. The incident was very much a 'one-off' and just exactly what caused it remains a mystery. Is it possible that two people can share the same hallucination? If it was not hallucination, but a kind of haunting, why were these two men the only ones to be subjected to such a frightening experience? Or have others experienced something similar but been too frightened to tell? Is it likely to happen again?

The two young men were travelling back to Annan late at night and the road was very quiet. They were some ten or so miles from Annan when the driver noticed the figure of a woman gesticulating wildly in the beam of the car's headlights. He was just about to swerve to avoid knocking her down when she vanished. The passenger had seen the woman too.

Hardly had the old woman disappeared than the two incredulous passengers were stunned by the sight of a crowd of murky figures apparently rushing towards the car. The figures were mostly those of animals – dogs, cats, farmyard creatures, animals of all sorts, both identifiable and unfamiliar. Amongst the animals was the figure of an old man. His long white hair streamed out behind him as he ran and his mouth was wide open in a soundless scream.

The driver swerved this way and that trying to avoid the creatures in this strange parade, but before long he realised that whichever way he turned, none of the animals was touching the car. Were they figments of his imagination? One glance at his terrified passenger told him that they were not.

The next moment, the air in the car turned deathly cold. The driver could feel some unseen force taking the steering wheel, trying to wrestle it from his grip and make him lose control of the car. In spite of the chilling atmosphere, the two men felt as if they were suffocating. One of them opened a window. Searingly cold air rushed into the car, accompanied by eerie, menacing sounds of cackling and screeching.

The driver put his foot on the brakes, unable to continue any longer. Invisible sinister presences outside then began to rock the car violently back and forth – the men were thrown from side to side, backwards and forwards. Finally, unable to bear it any longer, one of them threw open the door, ready to flee. As he got to his feet outside the car, all went quiet. There was nothing to see, and all he could hear was the sound of the wind rustling gently in the trees and the rasping pant of his own panic-stricken breathing.

The experience had been so awful and so exhausting that the two young men stood outside and took some time to gather their wits before they got back into the car. The driver started the engine again. Both men were by this time desperate to get home. No sooner had they started the car than the ghostly animals reappeared, swarming round the vehicle, emitting unearthly noises. The driver grimly held on to the wheel and steered a straight path through them.

They were nearer to home now. Surely it would all end soon. It was reassuring to notice that at last there was another vehicle some distance in front of them on the road. They could see its lights glowing in the darkness, and from its size and shape it looked like a furniture van.

Some yards farther along the road, the driver realised that the van was not moving. He willed his foot to press on the brake, but in spite of himself, he pressed down hard on the accelerator instead. They were going to crash!

Unable to prevent the inevitable happening, both men waited, wide-eyed, for the moment of impact. A fraction of a second before the car hit the van, however, the van disappeared. The driver found that once again he could control his feet on the pedals. The old man, the ghostly menagerie and the van had all vanished. The road was quiet and empty, and at last everything had returned to normal.

Completely drained by the experience, the two men made for home.

Ben MacDuibh

Ben MacDuibh in the Cairngorms is a magnificent but lonely place to experience a ghost. Upper slopes of the mountain have snow on them for several months of the year and make an awesome sight, but even in summer the landscape possesses a certain power. The mountain is one of Scotland's Munros (hills over three thousand feet high) and is popular with walkers and climbers, but in spite of that it is still very isolated. It quite possible for the solitary walker to spend several hours on the mountain without coming into contact with another human being. On occasion lone walkers have found that they have company after all – not human company but that of An Fear Liath Mhor – the Big Grey Man of Ben MacDuibh.

Sights and sounds of the Big Grey Man have been reported for more than a century now by several people. The ghost is not only seen on the mountain itself but also in the surrounding area of the Cairngorms, in the Lairig Ghru and in Glen Derry, for example.

Several common elements link the stories that have been told by various witnesses. One of the first reported experiences was that of Professor Norman Collie from London. He was climbing back down from the summit in 1891 when he heard something behind him in the mist. It sounded as if something or someone was following him down the mountain, taking one step to every three or four of his. Professor Collie was unable to make out anything in particular, as visibility was very poor, but he was sufficiently frightened to take flight, risking a fall rather than be caught by his pursuer.

Other witnesses in the years that have followed have told stories that have strikingly common elements about them.

Often the first thing that the witness notices is the sound of footsteps; the footsteps are heavy and slower than those of a walker of average stature. This leads the witness to conclude that what he or she is hearing is probably a very large person. Sometimes this is all that the witness has experienced. Other witnesses, however, have also seen something – generally a very large, upright figure in the distance. People who have seen the figure and have tried to follow it have seen no trace of footprints. Descriptions of the figure vary slightly, but it is usually described as being grey, very tall, human in form, but somehow not quite right – unnatural.

In 1943 a man called Alexander Tewnion was on Ben MacDuibh. He was a naturalist with considerable experience in the mountains. As he climbed, he became aware of the sound of heavy, slow footsteps. After a while a large figure rushed at him out of the mist. Tewnion shot at the shape three times but seemed neither to hurt it nor scare it off. He turned and fled and eventually managed to shake off his sinister follower.

The figure on Ben MacDuibh, whoever or whatever it might be, certainly seems to be a malign presence and its manifestations have succeeded in inspiring great fear in even the most hardened mountaineers.

Discovery, Dundee

Discovery Point, berth of Captain Robert Scott's ship, *Discovery*, is now a tourist site of which the city of Dundee can be justifiably proud. The vessel was built in the city at the end of the nineteenth century, and it is a testament to the fine workmanship of its construction that it survived the rigours of its service as a royal research ship in the polar regions.

On the British National Antarctic Expedition in 1901, *Discovery* saw two tragic deaths among those who sailed on her. Just as the ship was leaving New Zealand, a seaman called Charles Bonner fell to his death from the crow's nest of the vessel. The other death occurred some months later in Antarctica when another seaman was killed onshore.

It is the ghost of Charles Bonner, the first to die, that is thought by some to be the most likely cause of strange noises that haunt the vessel. The noises are heard above the officers' wardroom, just below the spot where the seaman fell to his death. Some visitors report a feeling of distinct uneasiness in the wardroom, as if there is a sinister presence there.

Some people also believe that *Discovery* is haunted by the grudge-bearing spirit of Ernest Shackleton, who embarked upon the expedition with Scott but was invalided out with illness and exhaustion. During the expedition, there had been serious personality clashes between Scott and Shackleton, and Shackleton was extremely bitter at being sent home.

Dunphail

The railway station at Dunphail is no longer in existence, but many years ago Dunphail was a stop on the old Highland Line. It was close to the station, in 1921, that the first recorded sighting of a ghost train happened. The man who saw the train was called John McDonald. The sighting took place on New Year's Eve. The time of the sighting, given the habits and traditions of the Scots, might have made people wonder whether the witness's mind was befuddled by drink, but it is reported that this was not the case and since that date, subsequent sightings have borne out John's story.

It was an alarming sight. The last train of the night had long gone, so to see one at all was a shock. But the strangest and most disturbing thing about it all was that although there were lights on in the carriages and steam billowed out of the funnel of the train, there appeared to be no passengers aboard. Nor was there any sign of a driver or engineer in the cab at the front.

The site where the railway track once was can be perilous for the innocent walker. People are reported to have been knocked flat by some immense and invisible force as they strolled along. The ghost train travels on, heedless of those who might stand in its way.

East Kilbride

East Kilbride, situated just to the southeast of Glasgow, was a pioneering new town when it first came into existence in the 1960s. But the ghost that is said to haunt the streets of East Kilbride comes from a much earlier time.

Jenny Cameron came from the Highlands and was a fervent Jacobite. She was a well-known figure who earned a certain notoriety around the time of the 1745 rebellion on account of the strength of her beliefs and her willingness to fight for them. Jenny Cameron was detested by the English, who circulated many an unpleasant story about her life and her wanton ways. These stories were probably completely unfounded, but they can neither be confirmed nor denied with any certainty.

Jenny Cameron's courage, however, was never called into question. It made her a legend among the ranks of the Jacobites, many of whom she joined in battle.

Jenny originally came from Glendessary, but when the Jacobite forces were finally crushed, she realised that she faced great danger from reprisals by the Duke of Cumberland's men and left her home behind. She moved south and settled in the countryside of East Kilbride, where, having bought a large house that she named Mount Cameron, she took in orphans of the rebellion and gave them a home. Her life thereafter was very different. No more a warrior rebel, she became a respected member of the community.

More than two centuries after her death, the area is now transformed. Housing estates have taken the place of countryside, and tarmac and concrete have replaced grass and rolling fields. Nonetheless, it seems that Jenny Cameron still feels quite at home and regularly makes her presence felt around the place where she once lived in East Kilbride. A hovering light has been seen by her grave on several occasions. Locals are well acquainted with her presence and feel quite comfortable with her.

The Flannan Isles

Lighthouses nowadays are operated automatically, but there was a time not so long ago when each of the lonely lighthouse rocks around the coast of Scotland had its light tended by a few stalwart lighthouse keepers. The job was vital to the safety of ships in the area, but it had considerable hazards. The job of a lighthouse keeper was a very lonely one and not for the faint-hearted – they could be isolated for weeks at a time.

Eilean Mor Lighthouse, off the island of Lewis in the Outer Hebrides, was manned by three people, a head keeper and two others. As they were confined for lengthy periods of time without other human company, they had to get along with each other or life could be very uncomfortable indeed.

In 1900 the head lighthouse keeper was a man called Thomas Marshall. His two crew were called James Ducat and Donald McArthur. In December 1900, their unexplained disappearance was to cause great consternation and speculation.

It was on 15 December that it first became obvious that something was wrong at the lighthouse. It was reported to the authorities that the light at Eilean Mor, which was supposed to burn constantly, had gone out. This posed a great danger to shipping in the area, and when the light had still not gone back on after a few days, a vessel was sent to the rock to investigate. A dinghy from the vessel was launched with a landing party, which tied up at the rock in an atmosphere of eerie silence. Why had no one come down to meet them?

The explanation became all too clear when the party entered the lighthouse itself. The place was absolutely empty. The lighthouse crew had gone. The landing party looked around for some explanation but could find none. There was no sign of there having been any disturbance. Everything was tidy and seemed to be in order, but the crew's outdoor gear, their oilskins and boots, were nowhere in evidence. Apart from the fact that the men had gone, the only strange thing that the landing party noticed was a piece of seaweed lying on the stairway, a kind that none of them had ever seen before.

It was unthinkable that the men in a lighthouse crew should ever abandon their posts. Why and where had they gone?

The log that was kept at the lighthouse gave strong indications that all had not been well before the men disappeared. On 12 December Thomas Marshall had written:

> 'Gale N by NW. Sea lashed to fury. Never seen such a storm. Waves very high. Tearing at lighthouse. Everything shipshape. James Ducat irritable.'

Another entry for the same day read:

> 'Storm still raging, wind steady. Stormbound. Cannot go out. Ship passing sounding foghorn. Could see lights of cabins. Ducat quiet. Donald McArthur crying.'

Tension among the lighthouse crew was given further mention on 13 December:

'Storm continued through night. Wind shifted W by N. Ducat quiet. McArthur praying.'

Marshall made another entry that day:

'Noon, grey daylight. Me, Ducat and McArthur prayed.'

There were no entries in the log for the following day. On 15 December the final entry in the book read as follows:

'Storm ended. Sea calm. God is over all.'

Several things were disturbing about the entries in the log. First of all, there were the mentions of Ducat and McArthur behaving as if something was wrong. Were they unwell or frightened? Was it just the storm or something else?

Then there was the fact that there had been no entry made for 14 December. Why was that?

Finally, the storm that was supposed to have raged around the lighthouse rock for three days seemed very unlikely as on the island of Lewis, less than twenty miles away, there had been no sign of any such storm. Had the men in the lighthouse been imagining things?

The official inquiry into the disappearance of the lighthouse crew was unable to shed further light on the incident. Nor were the three men ever found. But many people thought that they had been subjected to something supernatural. People had believed for many years that the rocky islands around the lighthouse were haunted.

Further evidence had been submitted to the inquiry that had only served to deepen the mystery. On the night of 15 December, seamen on a boat in the waters around the strangely dark lighthouse had seen another boat, manned by men dressed in storm clothing, cut across their bow. The occupants had not responded to the seamen's calls. The only thing the seamen heard in answer to their cries was the sound of the oars as they creaked in the rowlocks. Was this the last sight of the men from the lighthouse or were the figures in the rowing boat merely ghostly apparitions? The answer will probably never be known.

Loch Skene

Hogmanay by Loch Skene sees the return of the phantom coach and horses of Alexander Skene, who lived in those parts around the end of the sixteenth century and the beginning of the seventeenth.

Alexander Skene was renowned as a practitioner of the black arts; he is said to have spent some years on the continent studying black magic. His gruesome activities while at home by Loch Skene were rumoured to include digging up the corpses of unbaptised babies from the nearby churchyard and feeding them to the crow that is said to have accompanied him wherever he went, perched on his shoulder. People were fearful of Alexander Skene and claimed that his imposing figure cast no shadow, even when the sun was at its brightest.

The appearances started after his death. The story tells that he tried to cross the loch on his coach and horses using his magical powers and that as he neared the other side he came across the devil. The coach then sank into the icy waters and Skene was drowned.

Mull

The island of Mull, some forty minutes by ferry from Oban on the west coast of Scotland, is popular with visiting tourists from all over the world. Some visitors to the island may find more than they expect during their stay, for they might come across the headless ghost of Ewan (Eoghan) Maclean, astride his horse as it gallops through Glen More. The story of the ghost is rather gruesome.

On the eve of a battle with the Macleans of Duart, Ewan came across a woman crouched by a stream, washing some bloodstained clothes. Ewan must have realised that this woman was a banshee (bean shi'th), a supernatural creature whose appearance meant imminent death. The clothes that she washed were those belonging to men who were about to die. Having seen the banshee, Ewan probably knew that his chances of surviving the battle were not good.

Nevertheless, he was committed to his cause and would not shrink from it.

The battle was fierce, and in the midst of the fighting Ewan was killed. He was beheaded by a blow so swift and sure, it is said, that when his head was severed from his body, his body remained sitting upright in the saddle as his horse galloped away.

Some say that the appearance of the ghostly headless rider in Glen More foretells a death in the Maclean family.

Pitlochry

On the road leading out of Pitlochry heading northwards a grim spectral figure has been reportedly seen. People who know of the existence of the ghost are very anxious indeed to avoid it, for it as said that those who have come across it and have been touched by its cold white fingers will meet their death before long.

Sandwood Bay

Sandwood Bay is a particularly remote spot in the far northwest of Scotland, a few miles south of the lighthouse at Cape Wrath. It is a beautiful place, but few people go there as there are no roads leading to the bay; the only access is on foot or by sea.

Several sightings of the same ghost have been reported since early in the twentieth century. This ghost is not a nocturnal, diaphanous creature at all. Rather, he looks so real that some of the people who have seen him have tried to engage him in conversation. The figure is said to be that of a bearded sailor, dressed in cap, boots and dark-coloured clothing, with gleaming brass buttons on his jacket.

Nobody knows who the sailor might have been, although there are theories that he might have drowned in the waters close to Sandwood Bay. He seems to patrol the bay with a proprietorial air, keeping watch on the few visitors – mostly fishermen and walkers – who come to the area. As he patrols the beach, however, the sailor leaves no trace of any footprints behind him in the sand.

Selkirk

This story, which comes from the Border town of Selkirk, tells of the strange disappearance of a cobbler. The secret of what exactly happened to him is known only to the dead.

The cobbler was called Rabbie Heckspeckle, and he was, by all accounts, a skilled and industrious craftsman, quick and nimble with his fingers, who shod many a fine gentleman around the town of Selkirk.

One particular morning, the cobbler was up before dawn, as was his habit, working on a pair of shoes, when a stranger came into the shop. It was unusual for anyone to come looking for service at such an early hour, but Rabbie Heckspeckle was a shrewd business-man and did not like to turn down any opportunity to make a little money. Accordingly, he greeted the stranger with his usual courtesy and asked how he could be of assistance. The man was looking for a new pair of shoes.

The stranger was well dressed, but he had a certain air of decay about him, and there was something in his manner that the cobbler did not particularly take to. Nevertheless, Rabbie Heckspeckle po-litely obliged him by showing him a few samples of his work.

The stranger pointed to one particular pair of shoes that were to his liking, and although the cobbler did not have any in the right size, he measured the stranger's feet and assured him that he would be able to make some in time for collection the next day. The stranger said that he would be picking up the shoes early, well before dawn, and the cobbler, although a little surprised, said that such an ar-rangement would be quite convenient. The sun had still not come up when the mysterious stranger left the cobbler's shop.

Rabbie Heckspeckle worked all day and long into the night, com-pleting the shoes for the stranger. When he had finally finished, the shoes were as fine as any he had made. Congratulating himself on a fine job, he turned in for the night, hoping to catch a few hours of sleep before his customer returned.

It was still dark when the cobbler heard a knock on the door, waking him from his slumber. Rubbing his eyes, he pulled on some clothes and went to let his customer in. The stranger tried on the shoes with hardly a word. They fitted him beautifully, but he was far from fulsome in his praise for the good cobbler's efforts. He merely tossed a handful of silver coins at Rabbie Heckspeckle, turned round and made for the door.

The cobbler was intrigued by this eerie man. He wanted to see where he lived. The man was certainly not a familiar figure around the streets of the town. Unable to contain his curiosity, Rabbie Heckspeckle set off to follow the stranger, keeping at a safe distance. He followed the stranger all the way to the kirkyard and watched as the sombre figure made its way through the serried ranks of gravestones to the far side of the cemetery. There, before the stupefied gaze of Rabbie Heckspeckle, the stranger lay down on one of the graves and disappeared.

The cobbler rushed over to the grave site where he had seen the stranger vanish. There was no sign of digging nor of disturbance of any kind. Where had the stranger gone? Hurriedly, the cobbler left a pile of stones on top of the grave as a marker and rushed off to tell everybody about what he had just seen.

At first, nobody would believe him. The cobbler must have imagined it. The stranger probably walked out the other side of the graveyard unnoticed. The idea that he had vanished into a grave was quite preposterous, after all. But in spite of all the ridicule, the cobbler persisted with his story, and after a great debate it was agreed that the grave should be opened.

The gravediggers were summoned and the coffin was disinterred. The coffin was then opened in full view of several witnesses. Inside the coffin they found the body of a man dressed just like the stranger had been and wearing a pair of brand-new shoes. The shoes were so beautifully crafted that they could only have been made by Rabbie Heckspeckle. The townspeople had to believe his story now.

Nobody really knew what to do next. After some debate it was decided that the best thing to do was to seal the coffin again and put it back in the grave. Time would tell whether the ghostly stranger was likely to put in another appearance in the future. But before the coffin was re-interred, the cobbler reclaimed the shoes that he had made. They were a fine pair, after all, and what use could they be to a dead person?

He had made a big mistake. Next morning, before dawn, the neighbours had a rude awakening. Sounds of a terrible struggle were heard coming from Rabbie Heckspeckle's cobbler's shop. Several people, who had all been disturbed by the thumping and screaming, ran to the shop to investigate. They could find nothing except a set of footprints leading from the shop to the graveyard. The footprints led right up to the grave that had been dug up the day before.

There was nothing else for it – the grave had to be dug up once again. When the coffin was lifted out and opened, the townspeople shuddered when they saw what lay inside. The corpse, it seemed, had got his new shoes back. There they were, on his feet, just as before. Of Rabbie Heckspeckle, however, there was no sign, apart from a piece of his shirt, which the corpse held in its pallid, decaying fingers.

Rabbie Heckspeckle was never seen again. The people of Selkirk were left to wonder, with fear in their hearts, what had happened to the cobbler at the hands of the ghostly stranger.

St Boswells

The ghostly figure that once haunted the village of St Boswells in the Borders is said to have been that of a minister who murdered his housekeeper, but details of the incident are not clear. The identities of the minister and his unfortunate victim are not known – nor is it known when the murder took place. The ghost, nevertheless, is one that several people are said to have seen over a period of some twenty years at the turn of the nineteenth century.

The spectre of the clergyman – tall, deathly pale and dressed in black clothing – was seen by a pair of sisters on two occasions in the late 1800s. On each occasion, the ghost appeared very clearly, walking along the road for a moment or two. The figure was visible for minutes only. Then, quite suddenly, it seemed to disappear into thin air.

Similar sightings were made by various people over the following years, and, each time, descriptions of the figure that was seen matched. He was reported to be wearing ecclesiastical clothing – a black frock coat, gaiters and a black hat shading his eyes.

The Tay Railway Bridge

The first bridge that was built for trains to cross the River Tay was long planned. The idea was first proposed by an engineer of the Edinburgh, Perth and Dundee Railway Company in 1854. Proposal after proposal was discussed and resisted by various bodies involved until, finally, permission was obtained to build a bridge in 1870. The first stone was laid in 1871, and the bridge was completed and opened for traffic in 1878. Its life was tragically short.

On 28 December 1879, the Tay found itself in the teeth of a raging gale. By early evening, officials were in grave doubt as to whether it was safe to allow trains to cross the bridge in such conditions. A train from Edinburgh to Dundee was due to cross the bridge and arrive at seven o'clock. At the Dundee side, hopes were high that the train had been stopped before it crossed and the passengers disembarked. The minutes passed by after seven o'clock and the train did not arrive. Staff at the Tay Bridge Station, hoping that the train had never tried to cross the bridge, tried to signal to the southern side, but communication was impossible.

At length, the dreadful truth came to light. The train had been crossing the bridge when disaster struck. The structure of the bridge had not been strong enough to withstand the stresses that the gale had caused. A portion of the bridge had collapsed and the train had gone down with it. Some seventy-nine people were thought to have lost their lives, but the figure could not be given accurately, for not all the bodies were recovered.

On the anniversary of the dreadful disaster, a ghostly train has often been seen to cross the River Tay from south to north, following the line of the doomed bridge.

Tomintoul

Not far from Tomintoul, a particularly courteous and helpful ghost has appeared to travellers in the area. She is reported to be an old lady dressed in a long plaid skirt and shawl, accompanied by a wee black dog.

In the 1960s, a young couple staying in the district on a trip that combined business with pleasure were returning to their hotel after a pleasant day's sightseeing when their car had a puncture. As they set about changing the wheel at the roadside, a little old lady approached them and asked if she could offer them any assistance. The young couple were touched by her kindness but turned down her offer politely. They had almost finished their task, and, besides, she seemed a little frail to be changing wheels. The lady bid them good evening and passed on, leaving the couple to get on with what they were doing. The job was done in a matter of minutes. They got back into the car and set off on their way once again. They fully expected to pass the old lady a short distance farther along the road and were debating whether or not to offer her a lift.

The old lady had not been walking fast, so she cannot have gone very far at all, but in spite of this, and in spite of the fact that there was nowhere else for her to have gone except open countryside, the couple saw neither hide nor hair of her or her dog for the rest of the journey. It was as if she had vanished into thin air . . .

SIGNS, PROPHECIES AND CURSES

The stories in this chapter are not, strictly speaking, all about ghosts, but there are so many tales of ominous occurrences of a supernatural nature that either foretell imminent death or coincide with a death elsewhere that some of them ought to be given a mention. Some of these incidents have already been featured in this book: the mysterious appearance of Mr Swan, the traveller who 'visited' his family in Edinburgh at the time of his death in foreign parts; the banshee who appeared to Ewan Maclean the night before the battle at which he met his death; and the drummer of Cortachy, whose mournful drumbeat tells the Ogilvy family that one of them is about to die. There are hundreds of similar stories. Indeed, most people have probably heard that similar things have happened to a relative, or a friend, or the friend of a friend, even in cynical modern times.

Along with the occurrences that foretell bad things to come, there are also stories of curses included in this chapter. For what could enable such terrible promises to come true if not some force from another spiritual plane? In some cases it might be argued that those who have been cursed, because they believe the curse to be true, cause it to be fulfilled themselves, albeit subconsciously. If you believe something will happen, you can make it happen. This may be true. If something is expected of a person, he or she often fulfils these expectations in spite of him or herself.

Nevertheless, there are stories of curses – curses that have been fulfilled – that are much more complex and far-reaching than any that can be explained away in such a manner. Is it all mere horrible coincidence that such events came to pass? There must be some doubt.

The phenomenon of second sight is also given consideration in this chapter – is it a blessing or a curse and where does it come from?

'Bonnie Dundee' – Ominous Sights

Two stories have been told about the death of John Graham of Claverhouse, Viscount Dundee, 'Bonnie Dundee', the persecutor of the Covenanters who was killed at the Battle of Killiecrankie, a landmark in Scottish history.

The night before the battle, it is said, as Graham slept, he was disturbed by two things. First, he saw a strange red glow in the darkness, which could not be explained by human activity. This same glow has been reportedly seen by visitors to the site on the anniversary of the battle in years since. Ghostly lights are quite a common phenomenon, as has already been mentioned, both as signs of approaching death (death candles) and as spectral 'markers' of places where bloodshed and death have occurred.

The second thing to trouble Graham happened towards the hours of dawn, we are told. He saw a vision of a man by his bed, blood dripping from a head wound. The terrible figure pointed at Graham and cried:

'Remember Brown of Priesthill!'

Brown of Priesthill was a man called John Brown, a Covenanter who was killed for his beliefs. It is said that when the men in the firing squad saw Brown's steadfast courage and unfailing religious conviction in the face of imminent execution, they faltered, and Viscount Dundee himself fired the fatal shot.

Graham was greatly disturbed by the spectre of Brown of Priesthill. Thinking (hoping) that what he had seen had not been a ghost but instead some devious trick by his enemies, he got up and inquired of the sentry whether there had been intruders in the camp. The guard outside, however, said that all had been quiet and that nobody had approached Graham's tent.

The figure that Bonnie Dundee had seen had been a sign – its appearance, along with the eerie red glow, foretold his death in battle the next day.

Another person, many miles away, had a vision to tell him of John Graham's death. He was Lord Balcarres of Colinsburgh, unable to join his acquaintance in battle because he was under arrest on the orders of parliament. On the night after the battle, he was roused from sleep by a sound by his bed. He looked up and saw his comrade, Viscount Dundee, standing by the bed. He rose to greet him but the figure turned away and then disappeared. It was only later that Lord Balcarres found out that Viscount Dundee had been killed in battle that very day.

Sir Walter Scott

Sir Walter Scott had a keen interest in the supernatural, and during his lifetime he witnessed a ghost in his own home. A man from London, called George Bullock, was appointed by Scott to take charge of many of the building works at the writer's home, Abbotsford. George Bullock died in London in 1818, while work was still in progress at Abbotsford, fourteen years before the author's own death.

On the night of Bullock's death, Scott told of being woken by violent noises in the house. Although it was the middle of the night, it sounded as if builders were at work. Scott got up to investigate, but as he made his way through the house apprehensively, sword in hand, he could find nothing to explain the disturbance. The house was quiet again, and there were no signs of any disturbance.

Later, Scott was to discover that the bizarre events coincided with Bullock's death in London. The ghost of Bullock is said to have put in an appearance at Abbotsford on a number of occasions since then.

Visions of the Dead in Galloway

Two stories that originate from Galloway in southwest Scotland echo the story of Mr Swan (*see* 'A Haunted Capital – Ann Street').

The first story concerns an old man, a smallholder, who was working out in the fields on the hillside one afternoon when he caught sight of his son below him in the distance, heading towards their home. The old man called down to his son, but obviously the lad was too far away to hear him.

The old man was consumed with curiosity. His son was a sailor, and the old man was sure that he was supposed to be on a long voyage, still at sea for some weeks to come. All the same, the old man had work to attend to. The potato crop had to be brought in. He hurried on with his task – the sooner he finished, the sooner he would be able to go home and see his son.

The old man had finished his work by lunch time. He hurried back to the cottage to greet his son and hear all his news. But when he got home, there was no sign of the lad. The old man's wife was preparing a meal for two people, just as usual. The old man asked whether their son had been home, but his wife said no.

The old man decided that his eyes had been deceiving him – he had, after all, been high up on the hillside. What he thought had been the figure of his son was probably just a passer-by with a similar appearance.

Some time later, however, the old man and his wife received the tragic news that their son had been killed overseas in an accident – at the time at which his father had thought he had seen him.

The second story concerns a boy who was staying with his grandparents for the summer. The boy was sitting outside in the yard one afternoon, whittling some wood, when he saw his grandfather come out of the house. The old man paused to watch the boy for a few moments, then, without saying a word, walked off out of the yard towards the fields. The boy remarked to himself that the old man seemed uncharacteristically quiet, but he was too absorbed in what he was doing to give the matter much thought.

A few minutes later the boy went back into the house. He was quite taken aback when he saw that his grandfather was there, sitting in his favourite chair by the fire. Hadn't he just seen the old man walk away from the house, dressed in exactly the same clothes? It was the strangest thing – after all, the old man could not be in two places at the same time. Had the boy been dreaming or had his eyes been deceiving him?

Quite unexpectedly, the old man fell ill that night and very shortly afterwards he died. The boy now understood that when he had seen the figure of his grandfather walking away he had been forewarned of the old man's departure to another life.

The Cursed Mill

Many years ago, near Newtonmore, there was once a mill that was said to be cursed. The curse had been placed on the mill, it was said, by an old witch who had a grievance with the man who owned the mill at that time.

The curse wreaked havoc for some years after that. The first miller was killed in a fire. His successor died of a sudden and mysterious illness, after which the mill was burned to the ground. When the mill was rebuilt, the witch's heart softened a little and she weakened the curse. Now the mill would be safe from further problems as long as it was left idle for one day every year. Woe betide the miller who dared to use the mill on the forbidden day.

Many years later, the mill was bought by an ambitious miller who wanted to expand his business. He already owned one mill and wanted to improve his prospects with the purchase of a second one. He did not hold with superstition, nor did he like the mill at Newtonmore standing idle when he could be making money from it. The so-called witch was long dead, and the miller could not see what harm she could do from the grave.

In spite of warnings not to do so, the miller prepared to keep the mill working on the forbidden day. Hardly had he set the machinery in motion than there was a terrible grating sound and everything came to a halt. The small amount of meal that had been ground was full of grit, and one of the grinding stones had, incredibly, broken into several fragments.

Unwilling to admit that he might have been wrong, the miller denied to all and sundry that he had had any problems. He quietly arranged delivery of a new grinding stone and carried on working for another year.

The next year the miller was still determined to keep the mill working on the forbidden day. But this time not one piece of machinery would function in spite of the most careful maintenance. Nothing seemed to be wrong, but, all the same, nothing would work. To add to his grief and frustration, the miller discovered that a sudden and voracious plague of rats in his granary had eaten all his corn.

The miller had experienced quite enough. He sold the mill, deciding it was better to concentrate all his efforts on the other mill that he owned. His troubles were not over, however. His first mill was destroyed by fire, and he himself took ill and died very soon afterwards.

The cursed mill was then taken over by yet another man, a kindly and earnest soul who had taken a young gypsy boy under his wing. They managed to set the mill to rights, and it worked beautifully, making them a good living until the old man died. The gypsy boy left to find a job elsewhere, and another miller stepped in to run the mill. Although the machinery had been well maintained and everything appeared to be in good working order, the mill refused to work properly and the miller was plagued with problems. The gypsy boy was summoned to give his advice, and much to everyone's amazement, with a tweak here and a twiddle there, he managed to get the mill to work. Nobody could work out how he did it. And yet, no sooner had he left the premises than the mill ground to a halt yet again. The miller threw up his hands in despair and left.

The gypsy boy returned to the mill to take charge. As long as he was there, the mill worked perfectly well and he made himself a good living. But after his death the mill fell into disrepair. Because of the angry words of an old woman, long dead, nobody else could ever get it to work again.

The Curse of the Ruthven Ferry

Many years ago the only way to cross the River Spey by Kingussie was by boat. For those who did not have boats of their own, there was a ferry. The ferryman lived in a cottage by the crossing, ready to carry people over the river for a penny, whenever necessary.

Once, when the weather had been exceedingly stormy and the river was in full spate, the boatman found himself to be much in demand. Communion was being held in the church at Kingussie and there was quite a crowd waiting to be taken across from the southern bank.

Seeing the state of the river and sensing the opportunity to make a sly extra profit, the ferryman instantly raised his price to sixpence. Some people, unable to afford such a sum, shrugged and turned back for home. Others reluctantly paid up, but one old woman stood doggedly on the bank, holding out one penny. As far as she was concerned, that was the fare for crossing the river and she would pay not a halfpenny more.

The ferryman was irritated by the old woman. It was pouring with rain and very cold, but he was in no mood to take pity on her. He told her that if she would not pay full fare then he could not carry her across. The ferry set out across the water, and the old woman was left on the bank, standing in the rain with her penny still in her hand.

The old woman took ill as a result of her ordeal. She had been a stalwart member of the church, and elders of the congregation attended her during her illness and at her subsequent death. The ferryman, taking one of the elders across the river after the old woman had died, found himself subjected to a ferocious tirade. For having been selfish and greedy in the extreme, for having so callously refused to take the old woman across to her place of worship, he would suffer from here to eternity. He would be deprived of his living and die an unnatural death, impoverished and miserable.

The words that the elder had spoken came true. Things took a bad turn for the ferryman when a bridge was erected over the river shortly afterwards. The ferryman lost his only means of earning a living and, now that he was unable to pay his rent, he lost his cottage too. He scraped a meagre living doing odd jobs for people in the district for a while, until one day, cleaning out some pigsties for a miller nearby, he mysteriously fell to his death from the top of the mill into a pigsty. When his body was discovered, it had been half-eaten by the pigs.

Second Sight

Second sight is reckoned by some people to be a gift, but according to others, in particular those on whom this gift has been bestowed, the faculty is more of a burden than a gift. Characteristically, a vision of second sight is something that comes unbidden, and when it comes it is often unwelcome. The things that people with second sight see, or at least the impressions with which they are left, are rarely pleasant ones. Some people who are said or have been said to have second sight may have only one vision in their lifetime. For this they are generally quite thankful. Others, however, have several episodes, whether these appear to the individual as visions, dreams or intuition.

The faculty of second sight is often one that is shared by successive generations of one family, and there are numerous accounts of Scots, particularly Highland folk, who have been found to have the gift. These people are, in general, very much everyday folk, with everyday occupations, who just happen to see certain things that others cannot see.

The Brahan Seer

The name of the Brahan Seer has been associated with prophecies in many areas of Scotland over a very long period of time. His identity is often confused with others in history who had similar abilities. Stories of his prophecies have been at times confused both with the prophecies of other seers and also with mere superstition. That such a man did exist is believed to be fact. It is not known, however, how many of the stories that are told about him are true or which stories might have been associated with him in error.

In one way the Brahan Seer was typical of many of those with second sight in that he had no aspirations to fame. He happened to be able to foretell certain things with accuracy, and this made him something of a celebrity. There are conflicting theories about his origins, but the most likely theory is that he became known as the Brahan Seer because he was a labourer on the estate of the same name some three hundred and fifty years ago. The Brahan Seer made many predictions, but two of them stand out as chilling warnings of the route that history was to take.

It is said that the Brahan Seer visited Culloden long before the famous battle where the Jacobite forces were routed, and that on walking through the area that was destined to be the battlefield, he stopped. Then he said: 'This bleak moor, ere many generations have passed, shall be stained with the best blood of Scotland. Glad I am that I will not see the day.'

The second prediction, the one for which he is best known, was made by the Brahan Seer just before his own untimely death, which he suffered as a result of his unfortunate gift.

The Countess of Seaforth had asked the Brahan Seer if he could give her some news of her husband, who was overseas in France. The Earl had travelled to France to attend to some business, but he had been away for a long time, and the Countess was getting a little suspicious.

The Seer was initially reluctant to tell the Countess what he saw. He tried to fob her off with vague generalisations, but the lady was most insistent that he tell her exactly what was going on. The Brahan Seer, so pressed, threw caution to the wind and told the Countess everything. He went into great detail about her husband's activities. Apparently the Earl of Seaforth was not attending to clan business, as he ought to have been, but having a fine old time consorting with another fair damsel. The Seer described the woman, the luxurious surroundings, and the obvious pleasure the Earl was taking in the woman's company. It might have been what the Countess had feared, but it was not at all what she wanted to hear.

So enraged was the Countess at what the Brahan Seer had to say that she vented her anger upon him there and then. She saw to it that he was charged with witchcraft and burnt to death.

Before he died, however, the Seer made his most astounding prophecy:

I see into the far future and I read the doom of my oppressor. The long-descended line of Seaforth will, ere many generations have passed, end in extinction and sorrow. I see a chief, the last of his house, both deaf and dumb. He will be the father of four fair sons, all of whom he will follow to the tomb. He will live careworn, and die mourning, knowing that the honours of his line are to be extinguished for ever and that no future chief of the Mackenzies shall bear rule at Brahan or in Kintail. After lamenting over the last and most promising of his sons, he himself shall sink into the grave, and the remnant of his possessions shall be inherited by a white-hooded lass from the east, and she is to kill her sister. And as a sign by which it may be known that these things are coming to pass, there shall be four great lairds in the days of the last Seaforth – the deaf and dumb chief, and these lairds shall be: Gairloch, Chisholm, Grant, and Raasay. And one shall be bucktoothed, another hare-lipped, another half-witted and the fourth a stammerer. Chiefs like these shall be the allies and the neighbours of the last of the Seaforths; and when he looks around him and sees them, he may know that his sons are doomed to death, that his broad lands shall pass away to the stranger, and that his race shall come to an end.

Such a pronouncement, so startling in its detail, sounding as much like a curse as anything, was hardly likely to save the Brahan Seer from his fate. He was duly put to death.

His prediction was to come true, uncannily accurate in every detail. The Earl of Seaforth returned from France in due course and was astounded at what his wife had done. He was even more disturbed when he heard what the last words of the Brahan Seer had been. The Earl of Seaforth died in 1678 and was succeeded by his son, who was the fourth earl. The family had their ups and downs but fared reasonably well for some years. The fifth Earl of Seaforth lost his estates and titles after the rebellion of 1715, but the lands were eventually restored. Both he and his son enjoyed wealth and position, and in 1771 the family was allowed to regain the title of Seaforth when his son was made earl. He was to be the last Earl of Seaforth, for the title died out when he did. He was succeeded for two years by a second cousin, who died in 1783, leaving the chief-dom of the Mackenzies to his brother, who was the last in the line. Three generations had passed.

The last of the Seaforth line was Francis Humberton Mackenzie. He was born in 1755 and became deaf at quite an early age as a re-sult of illness. He was not dumb initially, but over the years he spoke less and less, becoming more or less mute in old age. The words of the Brahan Seer were coming true.

There were four contemporaries of Francis, chiefs who bore the characteristics that the Seer had predicted. They were Mackenzie of Gairloch, who was buck-toothed, Chisholm of Chisholm, who had a harelip, Macleod of Raasay who had a stammer, and Grant, Baronet of Grant, who was said to be half-witted.

Francis Mackenzie married a woman called Mary, and she bore him six children in all – two girls and four boys. Francis must have had the words of the Brahan Seer ringing in his ears for most of his married life, for all four of his sons did indeed predecease him, the last-born dying very young.

Francis died in 1815, the last chief. His estates passed to his daughter, Mary Fredericka Elizabeth Mackenzie. Her husband, Admiral Sir Samuel Hood, had only just died in India, and when she returned home to take possession of her father's estate, she was in mourning. So a lass had, as predicted, come from the east. She was also white-hooded. Not only did she bear the married name of Hood but she was dressed in white widow's clothes. Mary eventually remarried, and her new husband took over the estates – Seaforth had now gone from the family.

The final part of the Brahan Seer's prophecy came true when Mary and her sister had an accident while out riding in a carriage one day. Mary, who had been driving the carriage, survived, but her sister died. The white-hooded lass had killed her sister.

The origin or cause of the visions that come to those with second sight is not known. In some ways, the Brahan Seer was not typical of most people who had second sight. First, he had several visions throughout his life. Most people who have second sight have few visions – many have only one. Secondly, the Brahan Seer used a white stone, probably a crystal, to help him to see into the future. With most other people, the visions that they experience come uninvited and unprompted.

Are the visions that appear to those with second sight things that come from some unseen external influence or do they have their origins within the psyche of the individual?

The fact that the visions are more often than not unwelcome and unpleasant – very frightening at times – must make one wonder. Is a vision of bad things to come in any way similar to the phantom funeral – a sign from the world of the already dead?

A ghost story that comes from the Isle of Skye suggests that some people believed such an explanation was likely.

Second Sight – A Ghostly Gift

This story concerns another seer, Kenneth Ouir of the Lews, and how he came to acquire his gift.

When Kenneth was not yet born, his mother was out in the fields one night when she saw the ghost of a dead woman. The spirit was soaking wet – her clothes were dripping – and she was clearly in great distress. Kenneth's mother realised who the ghost must be. The body of an unknown woman had been washed ashore nearby a few weeks before. The islanders had been unable to find out who the woman was or how she had come to drown but had buried her body. Kenneth's mother was very frightened by the ghost's appearance, but in spite of this she felt sorry for her – she was obviously very unhappy. She asked the ghostly woman why she was crying.

It turned out that the ghost was unable to rest in peace. She was a stranger to the Highlands, and as the grave in which she had been buried had not been bought, she had not got the right to lie in Highland soil.

Kenneth's mother wanted to help, and accordingly she placed a handful of corn from the fields on the woman's grave. This would be payment for the burial spot. The ghost was thankful that she could now rest in peace, and as a gesture of gratitude she handed Kenneth's mother a beautiful black stone with the following instructions:

'Give this stone to your first-born son on the seventh anniversary of his birth – no sooner, no later.'

The ghost then lay down, finally at peace.

Kenneth Ouir was his mother's first-born son, and on his seventh birthday she handed him the stone that the ghost had given her. From that day onwards Kenneth was able to see things that others could not and to prophesy events that were to happen far into the future. The gift of second sight was something that, in this case, had come from beyond the grave.

The Curse of Alloa Tower

Alloa Tower stands bleakly empty nowadays, a haven for rodents and nesting birds and a magnet for vandals who have left their handiwork on the boards that cover up the doors and windows. The dereliction of the place adds to the air of grimness that surrounds it, but its proud tall walls and castellated turrets remain intact, as if making one last determined stand against the curse on the Erskines, Earls of Mar, the family who once owned it.

Exactly when the terrible curse was first uttered is uncertain; some sources believe it to date from the sixteenth century. At that time the Abbey of Cambuskenneth was destroyed by the Earl of Mar, and some people believe that it was the abbot who pronounced the curse upon the family. When it was pronounced and by whom do not matter so much as the horrifying manner in which events followed to bring about the demise of the Erskines, exactly as the curse had promised.

The curse promised the following things:

- The family would become extinct.
- The estates of the Erskine family would fall into the hands of strangers.
- One of the Erskines would live to see his home, a place where a king was raised, ravaged by flames. He would see his wife die in the burning house.
- Three of that man's children would never see the light of day.
- The great hall of his house would become a place for stabling horses.
- A weaver would work in the chamber of state.
- The curse would only have ended when a sapling, an ash, was seen to grow from the top of the tower.

The words took some time to be fulfilled, but in 1715 things took a bad turn for the Erskine family. They were stripped of their titles as punishment for supporting the Old Pretender. Their lands were confiscated.

In 1801 Alloa Tower caught fire. John Francis Erskine, the owner at that time, had to witness his wife dying in the flames. This must have been a devastating loss to a man who had already known great pain in his life – three of his children had been born totally blind.

A few years later the great hall was taken over by a troop of cavalry, who made use of what had once been the great hall to stable their horses.

Some years after that a weaver who had fallen upon hard times took refuge in the damaged building. He continued working at his craft in the chamber of state in the tower.

Around 1820 the sign came that the curse had run its course. An ash sapling took root in what remained of the roof of Alloa Tower.

GHOSTS ASSORTED

There are some ghost stories that do not fit quite so neatly as others into any of the previous categories. They should not be ignored, however, and hence have been given a chapter of their own.

Two Dead Pedlars

Life must have been dangerous for the original travelling salesmen. Carrying their goods and their profits around with them, they were easy prey for robbers. There are quite a few stories from various parts of Scotland that tell of poor pedlars who have come to grief at the hands of ruthless vagabonds. Sometimes something remains to make sure that the fate of the pedlars is not forgotten.

The Schoolmaster and the Pedlar

In the early nineteenth century the body of a pedlar was found floating in the waters of Loch Assynt. The body had a severe wound to the head, and no one could find his pedlar's pack. Foul play was immediately suspected.

The pedlar had been a 'weel-kent' figure around those parts. He made himself a fine living selling his goods around the district and was thought to have been reasonably wealthy. Robbery was therefore the most likely motive for the attack, but no one had seen or heard anything.

As no evidence had been left at the scene and there had been no witnesses to the event, it was decided to resort to the old practice of 'ordeal by touch' in an attempt to identify the pedlar's killer. This practice had no basis in scientific fact but had once been widely used in Scotland as a means of eliminating suspects in cases of murder. Suspects were made to touch the body of the murder victim. When the corpse was touched by the killer, it was supposed to bleed.

All those who had been in the area at the time when the pedlar met his death were asked to touch the body, and most of them obliged. The schoolmaster in the local school, however, refused to take part in the bizarre ritual. He argued, most convincingly, that the pedlar had probably fallen into the loch and hit his head on a stone. There was no gain to be had from pandering to superstition.

The schoolmaster was an intelligent man with considerable influence in the community. It was agreed that his theory as to the likely cause of the death of the pedlar was plausible. Besides, there was no real evidence to the contrary. The case was closed, and the pedlar was buried.

Some weeks later the pedlar's brother came looking for him. When he heard the story of his brother's death he was not at all satisfied that justice had been done. If the pedlar had not been robbed and murdered, then where were his pack and the goods and money that would have been in it?

The pedlar's brother investigated the matter himself and at once began to suspect the schoolmaster. He seemed to have an awful lot of money, even for a man in his position, and his tastes were undeniably expensive.

The pedlar's brother consulted a man with second sight, and the man told him of a vision that he had had of a murder committed by the schoolmaster. This was not real evidence in itself, but the visionary was then able to tell the pedlar's brother and the police where the empty pack had been hidden.

The schoolmaster was questioned. Eventually he confessed to his crime and suffered the appropriate penalty. But the fate of the pedlar is not forgotten. The terrible deed on the shore of Loch Assynt is re-enacted in ghostly form every year. The sickening sound of a skull being cracked echoes across the water, followed by a splash and the sound of the culprit's footsteps fleeing the scene.

The Sanquhar Pedlar

There was once a shepherd called Gourlay who lived near the town of Sanquhar in Dumfriesshire. He was smitten by a young woman who lived in a farmhouse a few miles away. The woman's name was Mary Graham, and she lived with her two brothers, Robert and Joseph.

One night the shepherd went to call on Mary Graham, but as he approached the farmhouse, he was alerted by the sounds of a struggle. Deciding that it was better not to risk going straight in by the front door, he crept up to a window and surreptitiously peeked inside. To his horror, he saw his sweetheart and her two brothers struggling with a man. It was hard at first to make out who the man was, but as soon as Gourlay caught a glimpse of his face, he recognised him as a pedlar who regularly plied his wares around the district. Within moments, Gourlay saw Mary Graham and her two brothers beat the poor man into submission and then strangle him.

Graham fled back home, all thoughts of romance gone. He was horrified at what he had seen – obviously the Grahams had been intent on robbing the pedlar. What were they going to do with his body? It was too terrible to contemplate. He told his mother about what had happened that night and swore her to secrecy.

The pedlar's horse was found wandering around in the woods close to the farmhouse the next day. There was no sign of the pedlar or his pack.

Gourlay stopped visiting Mary Graham. After some days had passed, she called upon Gourlay to ask him why his courtship seemed to have ended so suddenly. Gourlay was not quick-witted enough to think of any other response – he blurted out to her that he could not contemplate a relationship with her after what he had seen her doing on that terrible night. Mary turned on her heel and left his house in a grim silence. Gourlay had signed his own death warrant.

The Graham family did not wait long before they got rid of Gourlay and his big mouth. They ambushed him on his way home a couple of days later. He managed to run away, but they chased after him. Gourlay fell into the river. He would have been swept away there and then but he managed to get a grip on a tuft of grass at the water's edge. The Grahams hurled stone after stone at him as he clung desperately to the bank. Finally, his fingers lost their grip, and he slipped back into the water and was drowned.

The Grahams thought that their secret was safe. They did not know that Gourlay had told his mother what he had seen. Shortly afterwards, Gourlay's battered body was recovered from the river, and his mother was filled with rage. Without hesitation, the old woman pointed the finger of blame at the Graham family. Unfortunately, the Grahams managed to escape into hiding and were never brought to justice.

The pedlar's body was found buried in moorland some years later. The ghost of Gourlay returned to the spot where he was killed by the Grahams to haunt the place. The cries of the poor man as he clung on to the banks of the river in the last moments of consciousness were heard in the same spot from time to time for a long time afterwards.

Spinning Jenny

A small stream near the pretty town of Ballater in Deeside has been named 'The Spinning Jenny Burn' after a very persistent and industrious little ghost that has haunted its banks for many a year. A small, bent old woman, she is seen to work away feverishly at her spinning wheel by the stream, oblivious of any mortal that might lay eyes on her. The ghost is completely harmless and has never been known to interact in any way with living people. Who she is, or why she works so hard, no one knows.

The Modernisation of a Manifestation

There are quite a few stories told of ghostly vehicles that have been witnessed the width and breadth of Scotland, and some have been included elsewhere in this book. None is quite as strange, however, as the story of a ghostly vehicle that changed with the times. The story originates in the Isle of Skye, where it is said that for many years the sound of galloping hooves and the clatter of wooden cart wheels would herald the arrival of a phantom horse-driven carriage to a house in a remote part of the island.

Some time after the invention of the motor car, the occupants of the house realised that they had not heard the coach and horses for some time. Then, one night, they heard another sound. Unmistakably, it was that of a motor car. The house was in an isolated spot and vehicles were few, so when the car's engine seemed to stop, the occupants of the house looked out of the window to see who had come to call on them. There was no one and nothing to be seen. Puzzled and a little disappointed, everybody sat down again. Then a few seconds later, they heard the car engine start up again. The noise began to fade, as if the car was driving away. But no matter how hard the people in the house peered into the darkness, no one could see anything.

Motherly Love

There is nothing on earth as strong as a loving mother's instinct to protect her children. The following story tells us how that instinct can endure, even beyond the grave. The story originates in Ross-shire.

There was once a crofter and his wife who had three children. They had little money, but the children had a secure and happy family life. Their mother saw to it that her little ones were always well fed and warmly clothed. The children's needs always came first. Then, one winter, the crofter's wife suddenly fell ill and died.

The crofter struggled to keep the family going, but it was hard to manage the land and care for his children all alone. It was not long before he realised that he must find another woman to take the place of his wife and care for his home and family. He embarked upon a courtship with another local woman, and before long the two were married.

It was a classic case of the wicked stepmother. The woman was prepared to enjoy the benefits of married life, but she did not care for the children at all and treated them quite cruelly. Come winter, when the nights were long and cold, the children would lie shivering in their beds in spite of the fact that there were plenty of spare bedclothes stored in a chest in the cottage. When the children asked for more blankets, their stepmother refused.

One morning, however, the children woke to find that they were no longer cold. Their bedclothes felt heavier and they were cocooned in warmth. Someone had put extra blankets on their beds during the night. The children were delighted; their stepmother must have relented. But their stepmother had had nothing to do with it. When she woke and saw what had happened she was furious. She took the blankets from the children, stuffed them back into the chest and secured the lid with a lock.

The next morning she was enraged to find that the children had extra blankets on their beds again. The blanket chest still had its lock intact. How had the children got in? The stepmother threatened and hit the children, but they could not or would not tell her how they had got the blankets from the chest.

Night after night the same thing happened. The children would go to bed with a few meagre coverings, but by morning they were always snugly wrapped in soft woollen blankets. In spite of all the stepmother's efforts, she could not get the children to tell her how this happened. She said no more about it, but after a few days had passed she decided to stay awake through the night and watch.

The children went to bed as usual, curled up tightly against the cold. Their stepmother went through the motions of preparing for sleep, but when she lay down in her bed she kept her eyes wide open. She did not have long to wait. She had been lying in the darkness for less than an hour when she became aware of something moving by the blanket chest. She peered across the room and could just make out the figure of a woman opening the lid of the chest. The woman took out a pile of blankets and carried them over to the bed where the children lay huddled together. With great care not to wake the children, the woman covered them up with the blankets, tucking the edges round their sleeping forms. Then she kissed each child softly on the forehead. As the woman straightened, the stepmother caught a glimpse of her face. It was the children's mother. The stepmother leapt from her bed and made a grab for the woman, but she disappeared into thin air.

The stepmother left the house the next day.

A Faithful Pet

Dogs are widely thought to be sensitive to ghosts. The following story, which comes from the west coast of Scotland, tells of a dog with a particular attachment to a ghost.

An elderly crofter was heartbroken when his wife of many years died. His two sons had grown up and now had crofts of their own to manage. The old man found his widowed state particularly lonely and hard to bear. His only company at home was their dog, which his wife had been particularly fond of. The dog pined terribly after the death of its mistress and would not eat for many days afterwards. At one stage the crofter feared that the dog might die, but after some time the beast seemed to rally and returned to its former boisterous self.

The crofter would take the dog onto the hillside every day to give it some exercise. The dog was usually very obedient and stayed close to its master, but one day, some weeks after the death of the crofter's wife, the dog ran off. This was completely out of character. In spite of the crofter's whistles and calls, the dog disappeared. The crofter waited for some time but eventually returned home. Some time later the dog returned.

This was to set a pattern for the coming weeks. Mostly the dog would stay in sight of the crofter when they went out, but every few days it would take off and disappear for as long as an hour.

The old man did not have the energy to run after the dog, but one day he followed at his own pace in the direction the dog had taken. Over the brow of a small hill, he came upon an astonishing sight. There was his dog in the distance, in the company of a familiar figure – the crofter's beloved wife. The crofter stood and watched for some moments, then the figure of his wife faded to nothing. The

183

dog, large as life, came bounding back when the crofter called to it. The two made for home, the crofter happier than he had been for a long time because of what he had seen.

The Black Dog of Tiree

Humans are not the only creatures to return in ghostly form after death. There are plenty of spectral animals to be seen around Scotland, especially dogs. The hounds that howl by the ruins of Buckholme Tower in the Borders inspire fear in those who hear them. Another phantom dog has been heard crashing against a bedroom door in Ballechin House in Perthshire. Tiree has yet another canine ghost.

Tiree is a beautiful island off the west coast of Scotland, blessed with long stretches of silver sand around its shores. On and around one such beach on the northern side of the island a ghostly dog has been seen and heard several times. The dog is large and black and usually makes itself heard first with a strange, hollow-sounding bark. It will follow people along the beach for quite some distance before it disappears into thin air.

THE WEARINESS OF
A GHOST

Wae's me, wae's me!
The acorn's no yet
Fa'en frae the tree
That's to grow the wood
That's to mak the creddle
That's to rock the bairn
That's to grow a man
That's to lay me.

INDEX